Compliments
of
Weyland
12/14/00

UNQUENCHABLE BLACK FIRES

By

Leedell W. Neyland

LENEY EDUCATIONAL AND PUBLISHING, INC.

Tallahassee, Florida

1994

Leney Educational and Publishing, Inc./ Cataloging-In- Publi-
cation data.

Neyland, Leedell W.
Unquenchable Black Fires/Leedell W. Neyland

205 pages

ISBN: 0-9641539-0-4   (hardcover)
ISBN: 0-9641539-1-2   (paper)

Library of Congress Catalog Card Number: 94-76316

Printed in the United States

Copies of this book are available from:

Leedell W. Neyland
2522 Blarney Drive
Tallahassee, Florida 32308
Phone Number: (904) 893-4333

            and

Leney Educational and Publishing, Inc.
P. O. Box 15157
Tallahassee, Florida 32317–5157

DEDICATION

This book is dedicated to the memory of 209
black brothers and sisters who perished
in the Natchez fire in 1940, and to
their relatives and friends who
have endured the pain and
suffering caused by this
tragic fire nearly
fifty-five years
ago.

AUTHOR'S NOTE

This narrative is based on historical events which unfolded in a racially segregated society between 1940 and 1942. There was indeed a tragic fire in a Natchez dance hall on April 23, 1940. Two hundred and nine black people perished in that fire, with devastating effect upon Natchez and surrounding towns and villages. Students from nearby colleges and schools were at that dance, and the author was actually one of those students.

While the names of people and places have been changed, and any resemblance to persons living or dead is purely coincidental, the fictional experiences of Raymond Miles and others in a closed Mississippi society are drawn from real experiences. With race, laws and southern etiquette defining black-white relationships, it is not surprising that the white police forces would frequently join hands with the Ku Klux Klan or other vigilante groups to ensure that black people stayed in their places. It was out of fear and the recognition of limited opportunities for economic and social progress that many black youngsters dreamed of one day entering the promised land of Chicago or California.

Raymond Miles enlisted in the U. S. Navy as his method of escape, but he found that black people were oppressed everywhere. His role as a mess attendant to white officers on ships was precisely the role occupied by the blacks who were privileged to work in the "big house" on the plantations. Like many others blacks, he endured the disadvantages, oppression and pathos of institutionalized racism in the Navy, while dreaming and hoping for a dawn of new freedom to come.

The reality of Pearl Harbor on December 7, 1941 and his burns in a devastating fire on the USS *Pennsylvania* convinced Raymond that black people were destined to be consumed in "unquenchable black fires." North, south, east or west, he thought, these fires will continue to consume the hopes and chafe the spirits of black people.

Approximately 40 years ago, the author sought to capture his thoughts concerning this period in fictional narrative. He chose not to use idiomatic or dialectical language of blacks in rural Mississippi; he avoided the more risque language of Navy life; and he rejected rewrites dictated by others which might have made the book more appealing and financially successful. The author emphasized instead his own emotions in a style that reflects his own effort to tell a story that is meaningful to him.

While the story begins in southern Mississippi where most blacks lived as virtual peons and had few rights that whites were obliged to respect, its episodes of racism are played out the world over. Whether in the Natchez fire in Mississippi or in the fire on the USS *Pennsylvania*, differences between blacks and whites are shown clearly, even in the shadow of death. In Raymond's story, blacks are trapped and consumed on all sides by the seemingly unquenchable fires of racial hatred, bigotry and injustice.

LWN

Chapter I

On April 23, 1940, the small city of Natchez, Mississippi received national and international publicity when 209 of its black citizens perished in a flaming dance hall called the Rhythm Night Club. One observer remarked: "Truly, it was a *black holocaust*. More than anything else, it represented the offering up of two hundred and nine black souls as sacrificial lambs to the evil gods of racial segregation in an unquenchable fire." At the time of the fire, Natchez had a longer history of biracial social patterns than any city in Mississippi. This was simply because it was the oldest. Actually, about one hundred years before there was a state of Mississippi, there was Natchez. Jean-Baptiste LeMoyne, Sieur de Bienville, established Fort Rosalie in 1716 for the express purpose of punishing Natchez Indians accused of murdering French settlers. The fort was maintained as a military stronghold of the French on the Mississippi River as well as a leading center of trade and shipping.

Natchez did not long maintain its position of leadership. Although it could boast of being the oldest settlement in the state and of its once proud heritage as the center of antebellum culture, modern technology and industrialization had by 1940 reduced Natchez to just another medium-sized river town. At that time, it was a city of 15, 296 inhabitants, 42.8 percent white and 57.2 percent black.

In many ways, the city looked backward instead of forward. Its leading whites endeavored to keep alive its Old South atmosphere by preserving traditional landmarks and attendant social customs. Perhaps no other city of its size in the South could offer to the present generation as many symbolic relics of a society that had "gone with the wind." The whole city and countryside were dotted with antebellum mansions surrounded by ancient moss-covered oaks and sweet-smelling magnolias majestically overlooking "Ole Man River" which lazily formed the city's western boundary. Visitors might be met by a black receptionist with a banjo around his neck, hat in hand and bowing politely, part of the attempt to evoke an antebellum atmosphere.

Each spring, tourists would take a pilgrimage through the historic city which led to no less than twenty-five colonial structures standing imposingly as memorials to a gone-but-not-forgotten past. Beginning with the Adams County Courthouse, built in 1819, tourists were certain to be guided through mansions like Conti House (1788), Hope Farm (1775), Rosalie (1800), Magnolia Vale (1831), and Stanton Hall (1857). With the exceptions of Rosalie (located immediately in front of Fort Rosalie), which was Georgian, and Hope Farm, which was a hybrid of English and Spanish styles, the others reflected the old Spanish architectural influence. This influence had been imported into the lower Mississippi Valley during the period of Spanish colonialism from 1761 to 1801.

2

One followed the route of the pilgrimage fascinated by the charm of the fine iron lacework, the narrow window facings, large chimneys, majestic colonnades, colored stucco and a multiplicity of geometric designs. Alongside larger mansions and picturesque structures, however, stood small shanties or dilapidated houses owned or rented by lower-class blacks and poor whites.

Strange as it might seem, at the beginning of the 1940's there were no districts in the city labeled exclusively white. It was said, and perhaps with a great deal of truth, that the richest white family in Old Natchez would be living within two blocks of at least one black family. No one seemed to express any grave concern about the proximity of blacks to whites. The physical distance did not matter as long as social distance was observed, as long as blacks recognized their alleged inferiority by conforming to southern etiquette.

Among the 9,500 black inhabitants in the city, there was a well-known clique distinguished by its wealth and formal education. So influential was this group in black affairs in the state that they made Natchez the so-called black cultural center of the state. Most of the members of this clique were light-complexioned people who evidently had a sanguine connection with the people in the "big house." Recognizing this fact, many *peuples de couleur* would boastfully trace their ancestry to aristocrats of French or Spanish stock. In earlier days, based on the degree of white blood, these people would be classified as octaroons, quadroons or mulattoes. However, with time, black people learned to abhor these classifications and encourage the use of the terms "Negro" or "colored." This open attempt at identification with *peuples de couleur* was often suspect among many in the black community. It was general

3

community knowledge that fair-skinned people were endogamous, for families tried, with a great deal of success, to keep the color within the clique. But with the same intensity that families tried to preserve their color circle, darker men, especially, sought to break down the color barriers. As one ebony-skinned man summed it up: "Natchez is the one place in Mississippi where a man like me can go with 'white' gals and not put his neck in jeopardy."

Despite their clannishness, city progress dictated that people of color work with other blacks on community projects of common interest. In supporting Natchez College and in sponsoring cultural, intellectual and religious activities, solidarity among blacks was displayed. As long as such activities did not challenge black-white caste patterns, they received both moral and financial support from whites. One of the most popular cultural events was "Heaven Bound," a musical production featuring a chorus of fifty voices. The large number of Negro spirituals included in the repertoire drew many white people to the segregated audiences. The high point of the production came with the singing of "Swing Low, Sweet Chariot." For some reason, this spiritual appeared to have had almost universal appeal among southern whites. Presumably, most whites conceived of a chariot which would transport whites alone, or at least one with Jim Crow compartments. As the black singers looked out over their segregated audience, perhaps there was a latent hope that the chariot would bring whites and blacks together.

Like black housing, black businesses and professional services were located all over town. While St. Catherine Street was the main area of black business, some few blacks were reputed to own the buildings which housed large white businesses in the central portion of town. Often there would be a small black business on a very busy street dominated by large operators. Although most such businesses had to depend on black customers, some whites were counted as regulars also.

One physician of color owned much property in the central business district which was rented to whites. People talked freely about this man's lucrative medical practice which included among its clientele several of the most blue-blooded aristocratic white women in the city. These women openly recommended his professional services to others of their social set. The increasing demand by white women for his services finally aroused the ire and suspicion of influential white men who demanded that he confine his medical practice to black patients. Realizing that discretion is the better part of valor, the doctor gave assurance that he would conform to social expectations. Nevertheless, it was common knowledge that both men and women of the white race sought his advice. White men would dart up the stairs by night, to his spacious office, and house calls to imposing white mansions were a regular part of his evening routine. By day, he collected smaller fees from blacks who poured into his office to receive medication and professional advice.

In treatment of his white patients, the doctor had one socialized cultural norm in his favor—color. His identification with the black race was purely sociological, as he had all of the visible biological features popularly ascribed to white persons. This enabled him to enter places and households where those of darker hue in his profession were not permitted.

People with money, taste, and refinement, like the doctor, had won for Natchez the sobriquet of the black cultural center of Mississippi, but most blacks knew too well that the vast majority of blacks were excluded from the cultural activities of the minority. Like any other southern city of its size, Natchez had its sordid juke joints, speakeasies, pool halls, and call houses. These "dens of iniquity" were habitually frequented by winos, bootleggers, tinhorn gamblers, beggars, slickers, flappers and prostitutes. Since Mississippi was a dry state, the prohibition era never ended in most of its cities and towns. Perhaps there was not a still in every kitchen, but there were enough throughout the city and countryside to keep all the joints well supplied.

On Saturday night, these less inhibited souls from the city and untutored elements from the hinterlands crowded into these joints and gave vent to their pent-up emotions. In smoke-filled cafes or joints reeking with odors of wine, fish and flesh, half-drunken men and women lived it up. They drank bootleg liquor, ate fried fish sandwiches, and danced when someone played the piccolo or guitar. There was a special affinity for slow blues. As they danced to slow numbers like "Black Rider" or "Rock Me, Pretty Mama," expressions of all sorts would come forth. It always brought laughter when some uninhibited couple assumed the center of the floor and gave full suggestion of natural expectations in their dance. In such a case, it was not uncommon to hear someone yell: "Beef it to me, mama; I don't like pork nohow." Most couples dancing under those conditions rarely moved more than three feet during the course of a dance.

Every joint in Natchez was well acquainted with Ma Rainey. Ma Rainey was a short, fat, retarded girl who obviously suffered from a glandular disorder. She had once been an attractive, brown-skinned girl with long, black curly hair. Reaching her early teens, she began to put on weight at an abnormal rate. Being retarded and forced to remain in grammar school with children smaller and younger than she, she was nicknamed "Ma Rainey." Ma Rainey soon gave up school for the friendliness she found in joints. At first, men sought her favors and she obliged them freely. Of the many words that Ma Rainey did not learn at school, "no" was one of them. While no one would own this short, two hundred and sixty-pound girl as his girlfriend, few who frequented the joints could truthfully say they had not known her by night; and none who had known her would deny that she was a good lay.

As the years went by, Ma Rainey lost her attraction because she was reputed to have the "bad disease." Men in the know shunned her like a snake, but Ma knew how to get her a man. She would enter one of her favorite joints and get the guitar player to play her favorite tune, "Shake That Thing." If by chance the music maker was not on hand, Ma Rainey would gain attention and sing herself. Standing in a conspicuous place, with face contorted in its most suggestive manner and her entire body quivering like a leaf on a tree, she would begin:

Mama's got a wristwatch
Papa's got a chain
Sister's got a baby
From shaking that thing.
O shake that thing.

After a roar of laughter and a call from the men saying, "Tell us about the rooster, Ma," she would continue:

The rooster chew tobacco
The hen dip snuff
The biddie can't do it

But he struts his stuff.
O shake that thing.

Having driven home her point, with a serious expression she would strut around with every pound of flesh on her short frame shaking like jelly. Upon completion of this act, she would shake slowly on out the door, frequently looking back over her shoulder as if to say, "whosoever will come, let him come." When some uninformed country boy would follow, the boys would laugh and say, "He'd better get some pills cause he'll soon have a bad damn case of the claps or pox, if you get what I mean."

Such was characteristic of much of the public social life in the city. There were few places that respectable people could go. Most refused to be exposed to what their less fortunate brothers called "living it up." Such an evening usually witnessed many being taken to the calaboose, some to the hospital, and a few to the grave. Good people stayed away from most of the sordid little joints.

That Natchez was a destroyer of men could be attested to by many rural fathers who saw Natchez not as a cultural center, but as a city of sin. One bitter father, Pat Miles of Corapeake, had lost his son in Natchez during the flood of 1927. His boy, Hosie, had run away from home hotly pursued by a mob after being accused of striking a white man. Hosie worked in a mill town as a chauffeur and handyman for the mill owner. Dressed in his starched and ironed overalls with which he always wore a dress shirt, he sported the black model-T around performing his chores, and white people would say that he was "getting too big for his britches."

One Saturday afternoon, Hosie drove the car down to the mercantile store to get some gasoline. About fifteen white men were standing around. As he walked up, someone said: "Here's the nigger who think he's straw boss. We should drag him out of that car and put him in a nigger's place."

Hosie did not say a word. He started putting his own gas in the car as usual. When this was completed, the storekeeper walked out. Hosie asked him to put it on the boss's account.

"Okay, boy," said the storekeeper. "Are they giving you a rough time? Well, they're not going to lay a hand on you while I'm here."

Unfortunately, the storekeeper was not around long, for duties called him back to the store. Hosie cranked the car up, but before he could move off, about five men had surrounded the car trying to hold it. As he pulled off carrying the white men with him, one man slapped him in the back of his head. With almost superhuman strength, Hosie let go his fist and sent the white assailant tumbling into the ditch. Then he drove to the boss's house.

Late that evening, a black friend came to the boss's house and told Hosie that he must get out of town quickly, because a mob was waiting to catch him when he started home. Since his boss was not in town and he had no one to protect him, Hosie took the car and went the long way home, escaping the mob.

When Hosie arrived at the farmhouse four miles in the country, Papa Miles rushed out and inquired: "Where in the world are you going with that car? You're going to mess around here and get yourself in trouble."

"I'm already in trouble, Papa. The white folks are at me. They messed with me this evening until they made me so mad that I tried to knock a redneck's teeth down his throat. I know I should have taken it, Papa, but I don't know what got into me. Guess I just got tired of being a coward. Give me what money you got, Papa, because I'll either have to kill or be killed. I want to get out of this town. I'm going to Natchez."

"Son, don't run away," said Papa Miles as he passed Hosie the last two dollars that he had. "I got a lot of good white friends in this town who will protect you."

"Papa, we never had this kind of trouble before. Your white friends have never had to make a choice between you and their other white friends. When the chips are down, white is right, and a nigger be damned. You didn't see how much fun they got out of torturing me at the store. Your friends and the law work slowly, but mad Mississippi mobs hang quick. I got to go, Papa, because I've promised the Lord that no mob will take me alive. I'll never give them the satisfaction of making me plead for mercy."

Hosie grabbed his old single-barrel shotgun and a box of shells and threw them into the car.

"Please don't take that, son. They'll kill you for sure," said Papa Miles.

"I got to, Papa, I got to. As long as a man is a coward, he has nothing to fight for. He does what others tell him to do. He kisses where it tickles and asks no questions. When a man fights, something has taken meaning for him. His staying alive and protecting what he holds dear is not dependent upon the good nature of others but upon his will to protect it. At this point, I'm trying to protect life—my life."

As Papa Miles stood dumbfounded, Hosie continued: "Now, Papa, don't you try to fight them when they get here, and don't talk rough, because I don't want the whole family to suffer for what I've done. Just tell them that I said I was leaving for Jackson. Now you know I'm going to Natchez. You'll hear from me through our cousin there. Goodbye, Papa, and tell Mama and all goodbye when they come."

With these words, Hosie cranked the car and began turning around. Papa Miles cried: "Wait, wait, I have something else to give you." He dashed in the house and took a bottle of turpentine off the mantel and rushed back to the car. "Take this, son," he said. "If they close in on you with bloodhounds, just rub some of this under the bottom of your feet and no dog can track you."

As Papa Miles saw his son leave, tears filled his eyes. Never before had he felt so helpless. He had just seen his oldest son forced to run away like a scared rabbit simply for having made the mistake of trying to be a man. He did not even think about appealing to the conscience of good men in the community or to the law for protection, for life in Mississippi had taught him that neither operates where blacks are concerned. Because he knew what Mississippi justice meant for blacks, he had adopted the traditional black defense—run and hide. However, to this combination Hosie added one thing that gave man honor—fight, if necessary. Pat felt especially ashamed, for he knew that deep down inside he was a coward, and had taught his boys patterns of cowardice as a matter of survival. He knew that he had robbed them by teaching them to stay in their places and accept whatever the white man meted out. Even dumb animals fight to save their young, but Pat, sorrowfully, was giving up his firstborn to the dictated patterns of segregation. White man pursue—black man run.

As Pat sat on his porch absorbed in his fear, he heard an old truck coming down the road. He knew that it was the mob. He quickly rationalized, "I know it's wrong, but when a man's been cowed down nearly sixty years, it's difficult to stand

11

up and start fighting overnight." Thus, he prepared to follow the line of least resistance—to grovel at the feet of "white friends" in the mob and ask them to spare his boy's life.

"Where's that smart-alec son of yours?" they cried. "We came to teach him how to stay in a nigger's place. Don't lie to us, old man, or we'll give you some of it, too."

"He been here, white folks," said Pat, "but he's gone. He said he was going to Jackson. He had his boss's car and took it with him."

"We'll catch him, old man, if it's the last thing we do. So if that little bastard comes back here, you'd better let us know or the whole family gets it."

"Yes sir, I will, I sure will," said Pat. Then he ran up beside a truck on which one of his white 'friends' stood. "Please, captain, if you catch him, don't let them kill him. Just give him a good beating, but please don't kill him."

At that moment, as the truck was pulling off, a blow from a rope fell heavily across his face and knocked him back on the grass. As he lay there, he heard someone yell: "If we catch the black s.o.b., we are going to stretch his damned black neck." The men gave out with drunken laughter and a rebel yell as they vanished from sight. Perhaps unconscious of Mississippi's notorious reputation for having lynched more blacks than any other state, they intended to add at least one more to this number that Saturday evening.

Fortunately, Hosie's early start and use of the turpentine that Papa Miles had given him enabled him to make it to Natchez. There his cousins, Zachariah and Kissaih Wright, gave him lodging and assured him that he was welcome to stay with them as long as he desired. They knew already that he could get a job Monday on the waterfront, for Zachariah's

12

boss had told him just that day to bring him a couple of good hands for Monday.

Hosie told them his story and they listened attentively. They sympathized with Hosie's plight and assured him that Natchez was nothing like the little sawmill town of Corapeake from which he came. "Niggers in this town don't take no stuff," said Zachariah. "They talk back to the white people anytime they ruffle their feathers the wrong way. Some jigs will fight in a minute and these white folks know it. So don't you worry here with us. You won't have to worry about being lynched. They ain't lynched a nigger in this town since before the war."

As Hosie adjusted to the big town of Natchez, he began to feel more secure. He changed his name and felt that the anonymity of the city would protect him from his angry pursuers. To soothe his loneliness, he took up with a group of hard-drinking stevedores who liked to chase no-good women. Before long, Kissaih wrote Papa Miles:

> Your son made it here safe. We got him a job and tried to be a father and mother to him. But for some reason, he took up with a no-good riverfront gang and, Pat, he's going to the dogs. He's drunk pretty near every weekend. We don't know what's going to happen, but we can see that whatever it is, it won't be good. We wish you could come and get him, but we know he can never return home. Guess we both will have to pray hard and turn him over to the hands of the Lord.

Pat stuffed the letter deep in his overall pocket. He dared not show it to Mama Miles. It would worry her too much. As he went about the farm chores, his grief was so great that it showed plainly on his face. Knowing Pat better than he knew himself, Mama Miles said: "Pat, you've been acting funny all day. You got bad news from Natchez when you went to the mailbox this morning, didn't you?"

"Yes," said Pat. "You just as well read for yourself. We saw our boy saved from the evil clutches of the mob, only to be devoured by Natchez, strong drink and Jezebels. I've been thinking, thinking seriously. What would have been better in the sight of God? A good boy lost to hate and evil at the hands of an angry white mob, or a bad boy, bad of his own making, lost to the evils of drinking and wild women? I'm not certain that I would not rather see the first one happen."

"Don't say that, dear," exclaimed Mama Miles. "You know he's young and foolish, never been away from home before. Maybe he will see the light before it's too late."

Unfortunately, Hosie did not have sufficient time to change. In early 1927, the angry Mississippi River rose to an all-time high and burst through the levee almost without warning. Many blacks on the riverfront were lost in what was deemed the worst flood in the history of the city. After an intensive two-week search by city and private officials, it was concluded that those missing had perished in the flood. Having been informed that Hosie was on the waterfront when the flood hit and being convinced that he had perished, Kissaih wrote Papa Miles and told him the bad news. Kissaih wrote:

> Cousin Pat, I regret to tell you this, but from all indications, Hosie was drowned in the recent flood which took more than two hundred lives. We have looked everywhere, but he can't be found. The last time he was seen, he was with that bad riverfront bunch and that's just where the flood hit.
>
> Somehow, I feel that I must blame myself for his death, because I couldn't keep him away from that bad crowd. I know I failed you in this respect, but God knows I tried. I know I failed somewhere, but I honestly don't know where. All I know, when he got a taste of what the waterfront had to offer, there was no turning back for him. I'm sorry to say it, but if the flood hadn't got him, it would not have been long before he would have run

himself to death. If we could have kept him out of Natchez, he would have probably grown up to be a fine man, but the city was just more than he could take. It had too many avenues leading to self-destruction. Hosie found them all. There's no need to come to Natchez, because there's nothing you could do here. I'll let you hear from me again soon.

Pat and Mama Miles read the sad news with heavy hearts. They searched the Christian upbringing of Hosie and concluded that it was good. They reviewed his altercation with the white men and his escape from the mob. That was bad, they thought, but a colored man had just as well recognize that Mississippi is a white man's country, and stay in a colored man's place. Since Hosie did not do this, he should have expected what he got. Then who was to blame? The city of Natchez was the answer. Papa Miles said to Mama Miles, "You know, that city of Natchez is corrupt. It has enough sin there to make most men yield to temptation. Offhand, I would say that it's the place that God gave the devil for a Christmas present. It's no wonder that you have some people living there who are so low until they would have to tiptoe to touch the belly of a snake. Guess all the temptation they offered was more than my boy could bear. If God be my helper, I will keep my other boys out of that God-forsaken city."

"Don't be bitter, sweetheart," said Mama Miles consolingly. "The Lord giveth and the Lord taketh away . . . Let us not be bitter, but rather, let us serve and praise Him like Job. The Lord knows best. He moves in a mysterious way. While we don't know why He did this, let's love and trust Him more than ever."

"You're right," said Pat. "The Lord giveth and the Lord taketh away. Blessed be the name of the Lord."

For a few moments, Pat and Mama Miles sat on the porch of the farm house in pensive quietness. Perhaps both were doing deep soul-searching on the responsibility for the presumed death of Hosie. Presently, Pat spoke up: "Sweetheart, I feel better already. When a man is burdened and his heart is heavy, there's only one thing to do, `Take your burdens to the Lord and leave them there.' I've decided to do that, and I feel better already."

Pat reached over and caught Mama Miles' hand and said gently: "Guess we'd better get back to the field. We must try to provide for the living. If God be my sacred helper, I will give every other child I have an education so he won't have to go to the sawmill, so he won't have to go to Natchez and work on the riverfront. They'll be teachers and preachers, maybe doctors. They'll have enough education to stay in their places and avoid conflicts with white people. They won't have to run before a mob like scared rabbits, because they'll know that this is a white man's country and there are certain things colored people must do. Professor Niles at the high school is a good example. He's been here thirty-five years. Everybody respects him. He knows when to say, `yes, sir,' when to take his hat off, and he only goes across the track on business or when he goes to the post office. He hasn't been in trouble yet. Yes, I want my boys to be just like him, and I'll work the last breath out of my body trying to make them so. God forbid that another one of my boys ends up on the riverfront in Natchez."

"I'm with you, sweetheart," said Mama Miles. "When I married you twenty-five years ago, you know I said I'd be a helpmate `til death do us part.' I meant that then, and I mean it now. If God gives me strength, I'll die if necessary trying to help you make our other boys men."

With these words, Pat and Mama Miles started toward the field, toward a particular spot which they called the "new ground," because it had recently been cleared of trees. To this new ground, they carried new hope. Hope that their sons would grow up like the professor whom they wanted them to idolize, with the intelligence to know and stay in their places. To this new hope they jointly dedicated their lives.

In the City of Natchez, many of the forward-looking citizens were extremely disturbed over the social life of the city. Although the city was looked upon as the black cultural center of the state, such a designation did not jibe with reality. The black leaders there knew all too well that there was not a decent place in the city where highly respectable couples could go for an evening of dining, dancing and relaxation. They knew too well that an evening at most public places was likely to bring them in contact with Ma Rainey and her breed. Thus, they stayed away.

Out of these deplorable conditions came a group which was dedicated to providing a place which could capture the patronage of upper-class blacks without excluding all the others. In 1938, a group of thirteen men organized the Money Wasters' Club. This name was chosen because of its appeal. It suggested that its members were well-to-do and literally had "money to burn." As one person put it, "If you can keep a man thinking you've got what you ain't got, you won't have any trouble getting something out of him."

It was more by accident than by conscious design that the Money Wasters' Club had thirteen members. Once the club was organized and declared its membership closed, it was dis-covered that the number was thirteen. One member recalls that he questioned the wisdom of closing the number on un-lucky thirteen and suggested raising the number to fourteen. A brief argument ensued, but the majority wanted to make believe that they were not superstitious. So thirteen stood. "On more than one occasion," he recalled, "I started to pull out because the number rested heavily on my mind. Some-thing kept telling me that thirteen's a bad luck number. I heard it all my life. I really believed that something bad was going to befall us, but I didn't have the guts to stand up for what I believed." On the other hand, the majority scoffed at the idea of thirteen being an unlucky number and made plans for pro-viding high-class entertainment—the kind that would draw the prominent blacks.

Starting in early 1939, some of the best bands in the nation were brought to Ed's famous Rhythm Night Club. Black citi-zens of Natchez were given an opportunity to shake happy feet to music made by Andy Kirk, Jimmie Lunceford, Fats Waller, Cab Calloway, the International Sweethearts of Rhythm and many others. The barn-like dance hall did not have much to offer in outward appeal, the interior was far from elaborate in design, and the fixtures were commonplace. Yet, the club began to draw more and more patrons from among promi-nent blacks because it was large enough to accommodate pri-vate parties and because it brought in high-class public enter-tainment.

The Money Wasters' Club decided to make the Walter Barnes dance a big success. Advertised as a barn dance, per-haps in keeping with the name Walter Barnes, group invita-tions were sent to the high schools, colleges, clubs, and organizations. This gave the idea to many that this dance was to be a closed affair. At the same time, posters were distributed in public places. The fact that so many thought that they were coming as a guest of the club perhaps accounts for the larger-than-usual crowd. In fact, it accounts for the largest crowd in Natchez's history. The fact that so many came, especially from the upper class, indicated that black Natchez was starved for wholesome entertainment. Capitalizing on the knowledge of the need for this kind of entertainment, the Money Wasters spared no effort to make this a gala affair. The decorations, the band, and the general atmosphere were set for an evening of fun.

Among the many dancers who were to attend the Walter Barnes dance were two young lovers, Raymond Miles and Jean Gravier. Both were students at Sweethill College. Jean was the daughter of a prominent family in Natchez, while Raymond was from a farm family near the river plains town of Stephenson. Raymond Miles was the son of Pat Miles, the father who lost his oldest son in the flood that hit Natchez thirteen years earlier. Contrary to his father's wishes, Raymond was in Natchez seeking worldly pleasures. From his earliest childhood, Raymond remembered his father saying that Natchez would destroy you, but he had never taken his father seriously. As Raymond reasoned, he was not there for immoral purposes, but for an evening of wholesome recreation. Nothing evil will come from anything like this, he thought. He was in love with a beautiful girl whose home happened to be in Natchez. Since when, he thought, is it a crime to love a girl who happens to live in Natchez? He was there because all the big shots would be there, and if a man wants to be big, he

19

must think and act big. These things his father did not understand. How could his father, a farmer from the hills near the Mississippi River, understand such things?

Much too late, Raymond realized that there were many things that his father did understand. His father understood too well that the "dens of iniquity" will devour you like a consuming fire. He warned Raymond against them. When Raymond erred and yielded to the dictates of love, status and merrymaking, he was forced to pay the price. In this case, the wages of sin was truly death. Death, as the fires of a black holocaust ran rampant through the Rhythm Night Club. Billed and begun as a beautiful affair, the Walter Barnes dance ended in a nightmare that was to haunt the lives of many for generations to come.

Chapter II

From the time the sun greeted Natchez until its dying rays were lost in the rippling waves of the Mississippi River, Tuesday, the twenty-third of April, the day of the dance, was a beautiful day. Where the sun left off, the moon took up and shone with a brilliance that could excite Cupid to action in even the coldest heart. To the Money Wasters' Club, which sponsored this elaborate affair, it appeared that God had ordained this day for them. A kind of reverence must have painted the countenance of every sponsor, for now, with beautiful weather assured, their dance would be the biggest all-black entertainment ever undertaken in this river town. For the first time in the complex history of Natchez many of the black bourgeois would be brought together for a social event. As one sponsor gleefully remarked: "If the weather stays like this, anybody who's anybody will be there." A few hours later, as the southern moon beamed down on the barn-like dance hall, his prognostication was verified by the composition of the crowd.

As the hour for the dance approached, the demand for ducats increased beyond the wildest expectation. The demand came not only from the social elite, but also from the lower class, many of whom relished the possibility of a dance with someone on a higher rung of the social ladder. As friends met during the day, the question invariably asked was: "Are you going to the Rhythm Club tonight?" Those possessing tickets would reply exuberantly in the affirmative. Those without tickets would inquire how a ticket might be obtained. The dance was not billed as a closed affair; however, rumor had it that only a limited number of tickets would be sold at the door. Furthermore, tickets were sixty-five cents in advance, and seventy-five cents at the door. Ten cents at that time was a lot of money to lose, and the strength of advance ticket sales showed the black citizens of Natchez to be thrifty people.

Perhaps the name of "Walter Barnes and his Band" created a great deal of interest, because it had been billed by the sponsors as one of the top bands in the nation. While this billing undoubtedly overrated the orchestra, no one could deny the increasing popularity of this up-and-coming "young man with a horn" and his group. Walter Barnes directed a twelve-piece band that was achieving great popularity in the South. Born in Vicksburg, Mississippi, he had moved to Chicago in 1923 and studied under Joseph Schepps at Chicago's Music College. There he developed into a talented baritone and alto saxophonist, and was equally expert with the clarinet. His artistry on the clarinet won him fame in some quarters as the "Negro Benny Goodman." His professional debut was made with the famous Jelly Roll Morton, but talent destined to lead cannot long be subordinated to others, and in 1926 he formed his own band.

In the heyday of the Jazz Age with its unprecedented nightlife encouraged by the Prohibition era, Barnes found an abundance of work in Chicago. He hit the road to the big time in 1927 when he played many engagements at the Dreamland and Arcadia ballrooms owned by the late Paddy Harmon of Chicago's north side. At these spots he was widely acclaimed, and attracted a large following among white dancers. Perhaps one of his greatest thrills, and one indication of his musical ability, was his being chosen to furnish music for the dedication of the Chicago Stadium.

As Barnes' fame grew among white dance lovers, blacks more eagerly sought his services. His first south side appearance was at the Savoy Ballroom, and the crowd was reputed to be the largest such crowd in the city. From there, he moved to the Cotton Club on the west side, operated by Ralph Capone (Al Capone's brother), and was featured for several seasons. Realizing the economic possibilities in the South, Barnes was probably one of the first top-notch band leaders to exploit the Deep South. Having been born in a section of the country where few big-name bands from northern cities appeared, he hit on the idea of making an annual tour of the South. Jacksonville, Florida became his winter headquarters from which he covered most cities and towns of any size in the South. He soon became the idol of blacks in the South, and the apex of prominent social affairs was reached only when Walter Barnes and his orchestra were playing. In each town or city, he would always feature local talent in one or two renditions, thus starting many well-known musicians on their careers.

The knowledge that Walter Barnes would provide the music for the Rhythm Club dance was certainly a tremendous drawing card. On the other hand, and probably more important than the pull of Walter Barnes' musical talent or the desire to engage in ballroom gymnastics, was the psychological fear of being left out. Absence from such an affair would be highly conspicuous and would suggest social ostracism by one's peers. Being left out was a fate almost as bad as death itself. Whatever the complex of motives that prompted this unusual interest, the sponsors realized an advance sale of over five hundred tickets. An additional one hundred and twenty-five were to purchase tickets at the door.

Two enthusiastic ticket holders were Raymond and Jean. For more than a week, they had been scheming to obtain permission to attend the dance. Both Jean and Raymond were students at Sweethill College, located about one hour away, and they knew that the paternalistic policies of the college would not permit them to attend a dance. The college was not opposed to dancing, but believed that dancing should be highly supervised. At each college dance, chaperones would circulate among the dancing students to make certain that each boy and girl were at least six inches apart. If not, a ruler was inserted between the couple and moved back and forth until the desired distance was achieved. This was the first warning. If the same couple qualified for the "ruler treatment" twice in the same night, both suffered the embarrassment of sitting out the rest of the dance and restrictions from at least one subsequent dance. Knowing that the administration of the college abhorred public dances because they could not be properly chaperoned, neither Jean nor Raymond dared to seek permission from the college. Instead, Jean decided to feign an illness and stay in Natchez after a weekend visit, and Raymond was to sneak out of the dormitory and come down with some other boys.

The plan was all set and it worked perfectly for both. Jean, who had not cut her classes before, had little trouble persuading her parents that two or three days out of school wouldn't hurt her. Raymond, on the other hand, had to fold his blankets and pillow so that it would appear that a man was in his bed. Since his roommate knew his secret and was willing to cooperate, it was not difficult to deceive the dean of men who made bed check at ten o'clock nightly.

All evening Jean had been telling her parents that she felt wonderful, but never said a word about expecting Raymond or going to the dance. Around eight-fifteen, Raymond arrived at Jean's house. Hearing the anticipated doorbell, Jean rushed to the door and greeted Raymond with an air of surprise loudly enough for her parents to hear, who were sitting in the dining room.

"Hello, Raymond," she yelled. "What brings you to Natchez tonight?"

Before Raymond could answer, the whole Gravier family was coming toward the front door. Raymond greeted each one politely, then proceeded to answer Jean's question.

"I came down to see about you. When you didn't show up in classes yesterday nor today, I knew it wasn't like you to miss classes. So I assumed you were sick. Was I right or wrong?"

"You were right, Mr. Fortune-teller, and I'm so happy you came to see about me, but right now I feel as fit as a fiddle. I had planned to be back in class tomorrow morning, bright and early. How did you come down?"

"I came down with Oliver Hasty and the boys. We borrowed our favorite teacher's car and made the trip in an hour and ten minutes. They're all going to the big barn dance—Walter Barnes and his Band. Say, if you feel up to it, maybe Mrs. Gravier would let you go over for a while. I would love to add another big-time band to my list, and you know how much I love jazz."

"What about it, mama? Can I go? I swear I feel as well as ever."

"No swearing in this house, young lady. Now let me think about it a minute." She and Papa Gravier conferred for a few minutes in the dining room, and then returned with this answer: "I shall let you kids go, provided you promise to have Jean back here by twelve."

Jean cut her off by saying, with a tinge of sarcasm, "Oh! Thank you, mother, Cinderella will be back before twelve."

Mr. Gravier, who was sitting in the dining room, had seen through the scheme so he yelled up front, "This all seems like it was planned to me. Everything's too cut and dried."

Jean had learned that the best way to handle Papa Gravier was never to talk back, so she ignored his remarks. She invited Raymond to sit down and she made herself comfortable on the couch beside him. Raymond tapped her on the head lightly and said, "Can't get too comfortable, little girl, I want you to go early with me so we can listen to the band even before the house begins to rock."

"Come, come now, Ray. You can't be serious. Who goes to a dance at nine o'clock in this town? The crowd doesn't start coming in until ten-thirty or eleven."

"The crowd, the crowd, why do we always have to follow the crowd? Why can't we be individuals, sweets? Just why do you hate to go to a dance early?"

"Oh, Ray," Jean replied, "You know as well as I do that no one will be there but you and me, and I would just as soon look at you at home."

26

Raymond prodded her, laughingly: "You know why you don't want to go early? I'll tell you. You're too well schooled in 'colored-ology'. You know, my people will gladly pay sixty-five or seventy-five cents for a four-hour dance—one-third of a week's pay for the average kitchen mechanic or maid—and go to a dance at eleven-thirty. That means that they get less than half of their money's worth. Of course, if you'll excuse the expression, niggers in Mississippi are so accustomed to getting half value for everything that they're psychologically unready to take full value even when they can. Am I right, sugar? Come on, tell me, sweets; you know I'm right, aren't I? You might remain silent, but deep down under that pretty skin of yours, you know I'm telling the truth."

Jean smiled and remained silent and Raymond continued.

"When we get a job, we do most of the work but get half the pay of the white man; in most schools we go half the term while white people go full-time; when we buy things, we usually get inferior goods at exorbitant prices; while we pay taxes on the whole city, we are frequently restricted to only a small part of it. Even that college we go to—the best black college in the state, says the white man—is giving us literally half an education—Negro education. The only time we get more than our share is when we commit a petty crime, speak up for our race, strike a white man or have some beat-up-looking white dame accuse us of rape or even reckless eyeballing. Then and only then do we get more than our share—more time in jail or more rope around our black necks. We never get full value for our worth in Mississippi because we choose to accept what's given without question—because we have no guts. We're conditioned to be passive and complacent. We simply take little or much, good or evil, depending completely on the benevolent or malevolent behavior of the whites. So I know this isn't much, but tonight, I'm gonna get every damned minute's worth for my money. Henceforth, now and forever more, I shall cease to think and act like a Negro Mississippian."

"All right, Frazier, Cooley or whatever sociologist you think you are," said Jean, "if you are through lecturing, through theorizing, will you give a Mississippi young lady fifteen minutes to get dressed and then she will let a "northern boy" escort her to the dance. With the exception of slipping on my dress and powdering my nose, I've been ready a long time. So if you're late, you won't have me to blame. I hesitated because I just didn't want to go so early, but anything to please my future husband."

Jean returned to the living room within minutes dressed in beautiful sky blue. Raymond stood up quickly. "Gee, sweetheart, but aren't you gorgeously gowned? Come here, my dear one, and let me have the privilege of escorting the most beautiful girl in Natchez to the dance."

"Just a minute, Raymond," said Jean, "I must kiss mother good night."

Jean went to the kitchen and received compliments from her father and mother and a smart remark from her little sister. Returning to the living room, she took Raymond's hand and they set off to the dance. The happy couple strolled arm-in-arm toward the Rhythm Club, fascinated by the brilliance of the moon and pleasant thoughts of what the night had in store for them.

At exactly five minutes before nine, Maestro Walter Barnes ambled onto the stage in a most nonchalant manner. The eleven musicians (one was absent), who followed him were clean-cut, well-shaved, and dressed in maroon coats and dark trousers. The maestro himself wore a white jacket and dark trousers, making it easy for anyone to identify him as the leader. As they took their places, Barnes nodded graciously and smiled at the one couple present, Raymond and Jean, and at the sponsors. Barnes' popularity was due to his own personality as well as his music. He was very approachable at all times and very accommodating. He seemed to play more for the enjoyment of his patrons than for the money he received.

The band began warming up. The absent member was away due to illness in his family, not because of any clairvoyant power. Later, it would be difficult to convince him and others that luck or some divine or intuitive power did not plan it that way.

When the clock struck nine, the band rose, and with a nod from the Maestro, it gave out with its currently popular theme song, "Marie." Other than the wives of the Money Wasters, Raymond and Jean were the only people in the hall. From the time they arrived to the actual beginning by the orchestra, Raymond had stood at the edge of the bandstand with arm neatly tucked around Jean, engrossed with the warm-up procedures of the musicians. How heavenly, Raymond thought, to stand and watch the great musical wheels in action. "Jean," he said, "You're a darling for not being late as usual. I love you so much because you try to do just what your sweetheart wants, even if it hurts." Jean blushed slightly as Raymond gave her a momentary squeeze. However, it was obvious that his mind was not really on her but the band.

As Raymond watched the band, he experienced contrasting moods of reverence, joy, surprise, and pleasant disappointment. He revered and idolized the musical talent of these accomplished artists; was surprised at the seriousness with which they performed their task; was joyous over having the opportunity to share this experience; and was pleasantly disappointed when he observed that they were apparently normal men. Somewhere along the line, he had developed the notion that all popular musicians were "hopheads," "gage-kickers," "winos," or morally irresponsible individuals who lived depraved lives. He conceived of bandsmen as men who were by choice epicures with a philosophy of life summed up in the lines, "A loaf of bread, a jug of wine and thou beside me in the wilderness; Oh Paradise, Paradise now." He saw them as men who lived solely for today, letting tomorrow take care of itself.

Such a concept of the life and philosophy of musicians had grown partially out of his limited experiences. During his first year in college, Raymond had played with the college dance band. His music instructor thought he was good and openly predicted that one day he would make the big time. When the college band played off-campus, members would make an effort to mimic popular musical artists. There was a general feeling among the college boys that one had to take a few shots before he could get in the mood to play. On off-campus dates, coke bottles generally became camouflage for strong drink.

Raymond remembered with deep regret the one occasion on which he had been persuaded to take some "canned spirit." He had been told by his colleagues that while he played well, his music lacked feeling and soul. He was advised that a little swig of good liquor now and then would provide that soul. Trusting the judgement of his musical buddies, Raymond took a large swallow. In this act, he immediately realized that a lifetime of temperance training by his father had been destroyed. He felt a stinging sense of guilt for having broken a vow to his father that he would never drink. This first experience with liquor became even more traumatic when he became ill, vomited on the bandstand, and was summarily suspended from participating and traveling with the dance band by John Chrusten, the faculty advisor. At a conference period with Mr. Chrusten, Raymond tried to lighten his own punishment by indicating that all members of the band drank. Mr. Chrusten would not or did not want to listen to his explanation, so he succeeded only in being ostracized by most of his buddies.

These experiences did much to frustrate Raymond's hope of ever becoming a jazz musician. He abhorred even the thought of becoming addicted to liquor or drugs, but inwardly he doubted his ability to abstain under the constant pressure from fellow artists to conform. The very pleasant sight of an array of normal men making music that increased the palpitation of the heart and started the joint a-rocking did much to banish his preconceived notions. How wholesome it is, he thought, to see sane, sober men at work making an honest living by honorably applying their talents.

After several instrumental chords of "Marie" vibrated melodiously through the practically empty ballroom, a shrill tenor voice stepped to the microphone and crooned with great distinction the unforgettable words, "Marie, the dawn is breaking." Only time was to tell that a parody would have been more realistic: "Marie, the sun is setting..." Those present were truly enraptured. The dance of dances had begun.

"Let's dance, sweets," said Raymond.

"No, no," said Jean. "I wouldn't be caught dead as the first couple on the floor. I didn't come here to 'grandstand' for anybody."

"But there are just a dozen people looking on," said Raymond. In the meantime, another couple stepped in the door and began to dance. Raymond literally dragged a not-too-rebellious Jean onto the floor. "Why, baby," said Raymond, "You are so self-conscious. You're as cute as a speckled pup, you're shaped like a brick outhouse, and you have the prettiest darn set of stands (legs, I mean) in town. Just what in the hell do you have to be ashamed of?"

"Shut up, Raymond Miles, shut right up, and I mean it," retorted Jean. "I don't want to hear a word more of that kind of talk. You're an honor-roll college sophomore, but you occasionally lapse into that old crude, back-alley talk, and you well know that I don't like it. You don't have one bit of respect for me, yet you say you love me."

"You know I love and respect you, honey. Please believe me when I say I do. I respect you more than I do any woman in the world. Only we have different interpretations of what is meant by respect. Disrespect of a lover always involves a third party. If I tell you you're damned beautiful and I'm crazy in love with you; if I kiss you like this with your back turned and nobody sees it; if I ease my hands in between us and rub your breasts like this; or whatever else we do when we are alone and nobody sees us, I'm not disrespecting you. Lovers, in secret, can say or do no wrong so long as the behavior is not destructive. So when you tell yourself that no one hears me except you, you'll understand how much I truly respect you. When I say to you secretly that you're damned cute; good as gold; sweet as a peach; fine as wine—it's my way of telling you, darling, how much I really love and respect you. Understand? Don't you believe I love you?"

"Yes, Ray. But I simply don't like that crudeness. I mean I like what you say you mean, but I don't like the way you say it. So please, dear, try to say it just a little more romantic. Try hard to make yourself see what a woman likes—subtle, tender expressions of love are what women like. So promise me, right now—I won't dance another step until you make a promise to refrain from using those uncouth expressions."

"Let's dance, baby," said Raymond. "On a stack of Bibles knee-high, I promise."

"Now that's better," said Jean, and they started whirling across the floor. No sooner had they taken a few steps than the music stopped. "Well, " said Raymond, "That's the price of waiting so long to make up your mind. Oh! We didn't even show our appreciation," and they led the sparse number in a belated round of applause. In response to this display of appreciation, Barnes led his band in the melodious and currently popular "Tuxedo Junction." All couples who were now entering took to the floor without hesitation, because this mellow tune provided a tempo to which all could dance.

The ballroom by this time was rapidly filling, and a glance toward the door showed signs of a never-ending crowd. Raymond thought to himself that the crowd was certain to be a huge one. As an escape from the sickening effects of the crowd, he had decided to reclaim his little berth near the bandstand and prevailed upon Jean to watch and listen with him. But Jean had different ideas. She wanted to "swing out" and she told Raymond so. So they began dancing to soft music designed to "send you."

As the crowd began to settle, it was obvious from casual observation that merely being there was the foremost thing in most minds. Certainly few heeded the wishes and expectations of the Money Wasters who had planned a different sort of dance. It had been billed as a barn dance or shirt-sleeve affair. This option had been granted because experience in sponsoring entertainment of various types had demonstrated that blacks never dressed appropriately for affairs. It was the vague expectation that most would be dressed in farm clothing and the others would not be overdressed, at least. It turned out that a few wore overalls and gingham dresses, but the vast majority disregarded the barn dance label and wore ordinary street clothing.

One properly dressed patron, disgusted with this behavior, was heard to mutter: "Niggers are a funny breed of animals. Regardless of what you try to get them to do, they always have to do differently. If you try to give a formal, they squawk like hell because you didn't say regular or sport clothes. So what happens? Some so-called big shot turns up in a light grey suit or a pair of slacks and a sports coat. Now, we give a dance with enough latitude for everybody to dress properly without a penny's strain and these damned stuffed fools come here dressed like they're going to church or some association or something. Why, why can't we do right for once? Just once?"

Raymond and Jean, who had heard this soliloquy, felt that it had been meant for them and them alone. They had known far in advance that this was to be a barn dance, and they had contemplated dressing as Farmer and Mrs. Brown. Raymond recalled quite vividly a dance in another town in Mississippi which had been billed as a barn dance and turned out to be everything else but a barn dance. When he arrived attired in barnyard regalia complete with multicolored patches, he was sorely embarrassed. He turned out to be a sideshow for men in suits and ties and women in lovely dresses. So this time, he had told Jean that he was going to play it safe. He had rationalized, and properly so, that at any black dance, whether formal or informal, you can't go wrong with a dark suit. Then, too, being a student at Sweethill College some thirty-eight miles away, he felt it too risky to come so far without being properly dressed. His determination to avoid being a spectacle led him to dress in his newest blue checked suit. His desire to conform had made him a maverick.

Jean for her part, observed how handsomely Raymond was dressed and selected a beautiful blue flair street dress which was a stunning match for Raymond's new suit. Her soft auburn hair hanging lazily about her shoulders immediately suggested evidence of the white man's exploitation of oppressed black womanhood. Actually, her grandfathers, both maternal and paternal, were well-known, upstanding white men around Natchez. One one occasion, she had shown Raymond her maternal grandfather and her pointed nose, large eyes, and heavy eyelashes were the "spit and image" of his. Jean possessed no physical characteristic to classify her as a black person. Jean's fair color never went to her head. Rather, she frequently used dark powder to give her a darker hue. This night, she remained natural and appeared more beautiful than ever. Once at the Rhythm Club, they found the affair was really meant to be a barn dance. Raymond pulled off his coat and tie, took two rolls in his shirt sleeve, and ruffled up his black curly hair. Jean pulled off her necklace and earrings. Raymond pushed them into his pocket and made his way hastily to the checkroom. As he checked his coat, he received a kind of sarcastic compliment from the checkroom girl who said, "Mister, it's good to see someone here with sense enough to relax. You know, I ain't highly educated, but I know I know how to come to a barn dance." Judging from her "Daisy Mae" farm costume, she was surely telling the truth.

Making his way back through the crowd to where Jean was waiting, Raymond saw many supposedly educated bigwigs, who, in the words of the checkroom girl, did not know how to come to a barn dance. How true, he thought, were the stinging indictments of the Negro intelligentsia made in the soliloquy of the unknown woman and in the plain, harsh words of the checkroom girl. Perhaps in this distorted culture, he thought, blacks simply haven't "enough sense to go to a barn dance."

Raymond made his way into the arms of Jean, who was waiting especially for this dance. Not that she hadn't danced with others and certainly she was not opposed to his dancing with other girls. But it so happened that the orchestra was beginning to play "Star Dust." Everyone who has heard this melody knows that there is something penetratingly romantic about it. Thus it was an unwritten code at black dances that in order to shun the temptation of evil, "to each his own" on that number. Jean waited as was expected until Raymond took her into his arms. As they moved slowly on the floor, she hummed and sang, almost inaudibly, Hoagy Carmichael's magic lyric. She sang not because she felt she possessed special musical talent, but because it was customary for the girl to hum or sing softly when that song played, with eyes closed and head lying on a sturdy shoulder. Perhaps this was symbolic of complete surrender, both body and soul.

By about eleven o'clock, the joint, in the language of the hipsters, was "righteous." Good times and merrymaking, however, frequently make one ignorant of imminent danger. Their vision obscured by the syncopating music and its effects, few of the dancers, who were packed like sardines in a can, foresaw any possible danger. Later, all who remained alive to testify couldn't understand how they had been so blind. Anyone looking soberly at the situation would have readily seen the impending danger in the mixture of corn shuck, moss, paper decorations, and tree leaves. In this setting were odd costumes, wine, bootleg liquor, lighted cigarettes, and three hundred patrons too many. From this combination anything was possible.

In all fairness to the sponsors of the dance and the management of the Rhythm Club, strong liquor and cigarette smoking were absolutely prohibited. However, the denser the dance population became, the more difficult social control became. Many of the professionals present, whose public positions had made them follow semi-Puritanic codes, saw in this affair an opportunity to let their hair down. Realizing that individual behavior and personal identity are frequently lost in the anonymity of a crowd, many indulged in behavior that they would not or could not sanction openly and maintain status. To what extent this behavior, which violated protective ordinances, contributed to the impending crisis will probably never be known. Perhaps some carefree, irresponsible soul caused this inferno unwittingly. Perhaps the culprit, who consciously or unconsciously started the destruction, perished at his own hand. There are many theories which might be offered, including arson by a jealous white lover whose black mistress had attended the dance with a black man. Many might be unable to place the blame, but the religious could find comfort in their faith that God would judge.

Until disaster fell, the night had been a gala affair. If one did not dance to his heart's content, he could not blame Walter Barnes. At that time, Patrillo had not unionized all bands; thus Barnes played continuously until interrupted. As he gave out with favorite songs, "One O'Clock Jump," "Jumping at the Woodside," "Tuxedo Junction," "In the Mood," and current blues hits, dancers were moved to do the "Lindy," "Susie Q," "Big Apple," "Trucking," or just "swinging out." Although many tried these fancy dances, the size of the crowd made swing dances impractical. Fast and swinging dances were reduced to slow drags, or merely standing in one small spot and going through the motions. As one dancer summed it up: "I've been dancing all night and haven't moved two feet yet."

Most people disliked the crowded conditions and dark corners, but others liked it because it gave them an excuse to dance close to somebody else's woman. If he could do nothing else, he could at least excite the imagination. When a shy or unwilling girl tried to free herself from the snug grips of an enterprising young buck, another dancer would inadvertently push her back into his eager arms. Only by angrily freeing herself from his arms or awaiting the end of the number could she escape. If both partners were willing, the stage was set for uninhibited, highly stimulating and imaginative dancing.

As Raymond and Jean worked their way through the crowd, they were shocked to see a highly respected doctor of medicine dancing disturbingly close to the wife of one of the local teachers. Rumors around town had it that they had been going with each other for years. They had always been smart enough to keep it out of sight, but in a small town, everybody knows everyone's business. Everybody apparently thought he knew about "Doc" and his sweetheart and talked about it freely. However, the teacher's husband did not seem perturbed at all and in fact, considered the doctor one of his best friends. Because the teacher was such a beautiful woman, it was suggested that he was afraid to question his wife for fear she would leave him. On the other hand, one had to wonder why and how could such a beautiful woman live with such an ugly man. Since he was not rich, the only excuse was that she either loved him or that he had what it took. Of course, if she loved him, she would not permit herself to run with Doc and if he had what it took, she would not want to.

Doc was a tall, handsome man who was always immaculately dressed. However, he had gained about fifty pounds in two years. The boys at the club used to say if whiskey doesn't kill Doc, fat or women will. His wavy black hair had a slight touch of gray in spots which made him a distinguished-looking man. His voice rang out with deep resonance and eloquence, but this characteristic was frequently destroyed by excessive drink. People were amazed, not at his drinking, but rather his ability to drink so much and maintain his equilibrium and composure as well as he did.

Tonight, whatever doubt may have existed about Doc's clandestine relations with the beautiful teacher could have been dissolved by one look at the couple. Apparently, Doc and the teacher had had one drink too many, or both thought they were lost in the anonymity of the crowd. They were seen dancing in a comparatively dark corner and hugging and kissing as if they were in some cozy hideaway. Doc was dancing with one hand on her hip and another around her waist and kissing her with increasing rapidity. Several couples stopped dancing completely and watched the demonstration. There were some who showed surprise, some who showed disappointment, and others who were happy to say, "I told you so." Neither Doc nor the teacher showed any awareness of being observed. Both were too involved with self-gratification, too preoccupied with giving vent to built-up tension to realize that they had become a spectacle. Already the confirmed rumor was beginning to spread, but many who would have carried it further did not live long enough to do so. The behavior of Doc and the teacher was duplicated by many others, but none attracted the attention they did.

Inside the dance hall, the motion of the bodies and compactness of the crowd made it excruciatingly hot. Outside it was crisp and cool as many spring nights are on the banks of the Mississippi. Raymond and Jean thought it was a pity that the pleasantness outside could not be brought in. The two large fans near the front door were going at full force, but the locomotion of the dancers generated heat faster than the cool air could be circulated. A mixed aroma of perfumes, smoke, liquor, and body odor could produce a slightly nauseating effect, but one soon forgotten in response to the music of the band.

Just before intermission, the crowd insisted that Barnes play, for the third time that evening, "Tuxedo Junction." Sensing the nearness of intermission, Raymond maneuvered his dance in such a way that he and Jean were near the door when the number ended. "What a relief," said Raymond, "To get out of that nauseating crowd. Let's go out, baby, for a breath of fresh air." Jean, who nearly always agreed with Raymond's suggestions, appeared rather visibly upset by this most appropriate one. Tearing herself away from Raymond, she said angrily, "Go on out and take your breath of fresh air by yourself. You were just claiming a few minutes ago that we never wanted our money's worth, but tonight I'm going to get every bit of mine. Remember, you prescribed the medicine, doctor, now you're asking me not to take it. So you go wherever you want to, Raymond Miles; I'm making my way back to the bandstand." Raymond swallowed his masculine pride and followed her quietly, and for some unknown reason, he did not feel the inclination to force his dominant personality upon her. He knew well that with firm insistence and a little physical persuasion, he could have quickly changed her mind. He knew well that Jean abhorred public scenes and would have gone to any lengths to avoid one. While his impulse told him to "call the plays," he decided to let her have her way just this once. Not knowing that this independent decision was to be her last, he followed her sorely against his will. Why? Why did he follow her? Was he rendered powerless to go out the door, even though they were just a few feet away? Had Jean's number really come up and neither love nor mercy could have kept her from going to meet her reward? Whatever force motivated Jean and Raymond to return to their seats near the bandstand of the ballroom, it lured and kept them there until the fire.

At exactly eleven fifty-five that evening, someone up front yelled, "Fire! Fire!" But being accustomed to seeing dances and social functions disrupted by fights, Raymond nestled Jean a little closer in his arms and said: "Don't worry, baby. Some blame fool is fighting again. As long as they keep it up front, it matters not a darn to me." Before these words were off his lips, he turned and beheld the front door, the only door, covered by a mixed curtain of flames and smoke being blown toward the center of the dance hall by two huge fans which had been placed near the door to keep the patrons cool. These devices designed to combat heat had turned on their masters with the ferocity of a Frankenstein and were making the hall a flaming inferno.

As the words, "Fire! Fire!" rang clearly through the hall and the flames began to assume alarming proportions, a peace-

41

ful crowd which had been brought together for an evening of fun and merrymaking was immediately converted into a panic crowd. They were no longer doctors, lawyers, teachers, businessmen, social leaders and college students, but panic-stricken animals motivated by the dominating instinct of self-preservation.

At first, Raymond felt no immediate fear. Prior experiences in panic crowds had conditioned him to behave fairly rationally during periods of crisis. Although he was only eighteen, he had grown up in a sawmill town and had lived in the "quarters" or houses provided by the company. On two occasions, he had slipped off and gone to the "beer garden" with his friends. On both occasions, the beer garden was raided by policemen who presumably suspected that gambling, bootlegging, and other vices were a part of the routine. Since raids were made periodically, nearly everyone stayed on the lookout for the police. It was said, with some validity, that just before the first of the month one could expect a raid. Since policemen's salaries came primarily from fines, they made sure that they would make enough arrests to collect ample revenue. The most gullible people and the most likely persons to be arrested were blacks in the quarters. Raymond had experienced two such raids and had been skillful enough to escape. When someone yelled, "Police! Police!" he effectively fought his way through the fleeing, hysterical clientele and escaped apprehension. He had also seen his home burned when he was fourteen, and while his mother stood horror stricken, he had made a daring rescue of his little sister. For this latter display of bravery, people in the community had heaped lavish praise upon him for his ability to remain clam. If ever there was a need for calmness, it was now. All the time, Raymond had confidence in his ability to extricate Jean and himself from this entangling web, and this confidence was further strengthened by the fact that he was a college football sensation. His adeptness in evading charging lines or penetrating holes in forward walls led him to have almost superhuman faith in his ability. He had this exaggerated notion that he could not be trapped. Perhaps this was the one thing that saved his life.

As the fire completely engulfed the front door and began its rampage through the decoration of moss, cornstalks, and paper, the panic-stricken crowd ran toward the windows on the right side. Perhaps all would have gone well had the windows really been windows. Instead, they turned out to be merely indentations in the wall. Previous experience at dances had convinced the management that many of the customers slipped in through the windows; thus, it had been found expedient to bar the windows to prevent freeloaders from entering. Several of the less sturdy windows were kicked or knocked out and many were able to escape. However, as the stampeding crowd reached the window, the survival of the fittest became the rule. One would actually pull the other back as they struggled to reach an exit.

Raymond stood calm and collected for a few seconds. At the outset he found himself standing opposite the fountain at the extreme back of the hall which could only sell soft drinks legally. Yet, there was evidence that wine and stronger drinks had found a point of entry. In those fleeting seconds, he observed the competitive struggle for existence waged underneath the windows. It was painful to see so many obviously losing the battle by being trampled under the feet of the fleeing hordes. Within a matter of minutes, he saw bodies, yet alive, stacked between three and four feet high around the windows. The screaming, moaning, and wailing were for some their very last expressions of emotion.

As the movement of the crowd threatened to engulf Raymond and Jean, without saying a word, he pulled her toward the bandstand and the two jumped aloft. The band instruments and sheet music lay scattered. Raymond remembered that the band had made a feeble effort to keep the crowd together by playing a few seconds of its theme song, but like others in a panic situation, they had fled. Standing there amid the results of mass confusion, Raymond, clinging feverishly to Jean, tried to formulate in his mind a rational method of escape. Whatever plans he laid were made inoperative by two negating factors. First, Jean, who had been incredibly calm under the persuasion of Raymond, now became convulsively panicky; and second, the lights went out. The roaring swells of fire and smoke reminded Raymond of a picture of hell he had so frequently seen in the family Bible. He remembered vividly how sinners who had not obeyed the command of God were running and crying in their efforts to escape the horrors of an eternal fire. He also remembered Dante's characterization of the Inferno, and he could see that many Christians whom he saw at church each Sunday would in all probability be consumed by this fire. A combination of factors caused him to pray, not so much for himself, but that Jean would compose herself so he could get her out.

The lights were out. Smoke was bailing up thicker and thicker. If one could avoid the fire, he was still in danger of losing his life by becoming asphyxiated by the heavy fumes. He could hesitate no longer, he had to get out. Jean had fainted. He picked up her limp body and started toward the front door. In the pitch dark, he first ran into a table, but it was not difficult to get around it. He recalled that while on the bandstand he had seen the door. If he could just keep his sense of direction, he would take a chance by carrying her under the blaze raging about six feet above. He calculated that they would get burned, but anything was better than death. As he reached the center of the hall, he was knocked to the floor by the terrific impact of the fleeing crowd. Perhaps the smoke was beginning to weaken him, because never had he been hit like that on a football field. For a while he must have lain unconscious on the floor. He had no knowledge of how long he was there. As soon as he came to, he thought about Jean. He clutched his arms to him, but she was not there. On his knees, he crawled around on the floor hoping that he could find her. He touched body after body, but he had no method of knowing which was hers. He called her name feverishly. "Jean! Jean, darling? Where are you? Answer me . . . please, please." His feeble cries were drowned completely.

On the brink of death, a few seconds can seem like an eternity. Love for others, while no less real, tends to be unconsciously relegated to a secondary position. Reason gives way to fear, and fear destroys responsibility to others. In these moments of crisis, of unbridled fear, man's irrational behavior cannot be rightly characterized as cowardice. Men who bravely face conditions which could lead to death at any moment in their daily routine certainly are not destitute of courage. When influenced, however, by the behavior of the hysterical masses, they lose their identities and react as the group. Not many men can face the imminent possibility of death calmly. Not many can find comfort in the omnipotent power of God to save as they face their Gethsemane.

Raymond, who was certainly no coward, felt no fear at the outset. He felt no fear when the lights went out. Supremely confident in his ability to evade a crowd, he was not at all fearful when he nestled Jean into his arms and started toward the door. Only when he discovered that he had lost Jean did fear begin to engulf him, to destroy his heretofore rational behavior. As smoke began to choke out every breath of fresh air, he, like others, responded solely to the first law of nature.

As smoke and fire whirled toward the distant end of the dance hall, Raymond could hear cries of, "Lord, have mercy. Oh! God, let me out!" Others were just screaming with little or no conscious direction as an inevitable but terrible fate descended upon them. Raymond called out, "Jean! Jean!" but his voice was weakening with each call. He said to himself, "I can't die here. What would my father think, finding his son dead in a dance hall?" Jean must be out, he thought, or hoped. At that instant, he looked up and through the rainbow colors created by fire, smoke, and water gushing through the window, he could see the door, the only exit from this holocaust. With all the energy he could muster, he bent over in a football pose and headed straight toward the door. He had a clear field ahead. The fire had removed all human obstacles. It depended on his reserve strength to take him through the beckoning door, the goal line of safety.

The dash toward the door was more like a mile race than twenty-five or thirty-five yards. Midway, a huge piece of flaming moss fell from the ceiling. Instinctively, Raymond threw up his hands to prevent it from falling on his head. While he broke part of the fall, much of the moss stuck to his hands, while some fell on his head and shoulders. Shaking off as much as possible, he continued running under the flame hoping to escape before his clothes were ignited. Suddenly, the door and the undecorated corridor appeared before him like the land of Paradise. Although weakened to the point of complete exhaustion, he found strength to say, "Thank God." He could not say why he did not stop as soon as he was outside, but for some reason, he ran across the street, past the service station and toward the white section of town. With clothing scorched yellow, hair burned off almost completely, face and hands seared by the intensity of the heat, and lungs filled with fumes, Raymond collapsed on the street. When he came to, he was lying on a couch with benevolent white faces looking down on him.

Chapter III

W ait just a minute, son. Hold still just a minute and
I'll take some of that fire out of you."

As Raymond regained consciousness, these words, spoken in
a gentle drawl, were the first he heard. Looking up, he saw
the kind face of a fortyish white woman looking down on him.
She was very pale and her straight auburn hair, hanging in
plaits on each side of her head, frequently disturbed her as she
applied medication to Raymond's burns. She wore only a
white, loosely-fitted outing nightgown which showed her
hanging breasts as she leaned over. Raymond saw in this lady
a respect for humanity which reminded him of his own dear
mother, who could easily forget herself in the service of
others.

"Where am I?" asked Raymond.

"You're safe, son. We're not gonna hurt you. You had `fell
out' out there in the street and my husband and boy brought
you in here. We're going to fix you up."

Raymond looked about the room. He saw two men and a
young white girl about fourteen. He immediately deduced

that they were all part of the family—the father, mother, and two children. Ordinarily, Raymond would have felt ill at ease to have a white woman working on him while white men looked on, but he could see compassion written across the countenance of each. As he lay in the white family's living room, he discovered momentarily a new world. He had conceived of all white people as the irreconcilable enemies of blacks—oppressors of their rights to life, liberty, and happiness—and he now saw before his very eyes a group motivated solely by humanitarian interest. They did not know him; he was socially inferior to them; it was against convention to take him in the front room and treat him.

"Am I burned badly?" he asked.

The white mother answered truthfully, "Yes son, you are burned pretty badly, but just be thankful to the Lord He saved your life."

She then looked around at her husband and said, "Papa, look in there on the mantle shelf and bring me some castor oil." Papa, who had been murmuring, "Lord, ain't that awful? Ain't that awful?" moved quickly now.

When Papa returned with the castor oil, Mama remembered that she needed baking soda. She turned to her daughter. "Sister, go in the kitchen and get me some soda, a spoon, and a saucer."

Taking her hands off Raymond for the first time, she went into her room and came back with part of a sheet. She ripped it into small pieces, put baking soda into the saucer, emptied the castor oil over the soda, then mixed it evenly with the spoon. She spread this mixture all over Raymond's face, hands, head, shoulders and back. She carried out this task in complete silence. The occasional tears which fell from her eyes onto

Raymond's body told him better than words how deeply she felt his sufferings.

After completing her first aid and wrapping cloths saturated with oil around his hands, she looked at his head once more to see if anything more could be done. All Raymond's hair had been burned off and the sight of his parched scalp was more than the mother could bear. She burst into sobs. "Such a nice-looking colored boy . . . I feel for his mother."

At that point, the father stepped in and made his wife sit down. He spoke gently, "Take it easy, Mama. Take it easy."

Then he turned to Raymond and asked: "Where're you from, boy?"

"Sweethill College," Raymond replied.

"How're you gonna get back?"

"I don't know, sir. We came in the car, so I'll have to go out and find the driver."

"You can't go anywhere like you are. Anyway, for all we know, the driver could have got burned up." Then the father suddenly realized that it was best that Raymond leave.

"As much as we'd like to, we can't keep you here tonight, can we Mama? That would ruin us here in the community. We could carry him to Susie Adams—I know she would let him stay there."

The father did not identify Susie Adams, but Raymond assumed she must be a black woman nearby whom the white family knew. Raymond sat up on the couch. All eyes were fixed on him. Before they could say a word, Raymond spoke. "My hands and face are burning, but otherwise I feel all right. I want to thank you for all you've done for me, but I believe it's best that I try to find the boys and get back to school."

Standing in the middle of the floor, he felt remarkably well, except for the burns. The mother buttoned his shirt. "Are you sure you can make it, son?"

"Yes ma'am," he answered. "Thank you again for what you did—for saving my life."

"Best of luck, boy. Hope you soon get all right. Good night."

"Good night and thank you," Raymond said.

Raymond walked out onto the street. He could not understand how he had gotten so far from the Club. Could he have run that far? Did he drift that far in an unconscious state? These questions he could not answer. Anyway, his attention was being drawn from himself by his intense desire to find out what had happened to Jean and his fellow students from Sweethill.

As Raymond walked along the street, many thoughts entered his mind—mostly bad. He asked himself repeatedly, "Did Jean get out?" While he hoped and prayed that she had, he was not naive enough to overlook the possibility that she had not. He wanted to ask someone, but he was afraid of what he might hear. Somehow, he had little fear concerning his colleagues from Sweethill, but extreme apprehension about Jean's fate. He thought, "If God would be kind enough to spare her this time, I would never leave her again."

As Raymond neared the Rhythm Club, he heard more and more clearly the emotional outbursts of bereaved and anxious relatives. A large woman passed him running and screaming, "Oh God! I must get there. My baby is in there." Her behavior moved Raymond to action. He broke into a trot. Perhaps he, too, had been crying aloud without realizing it.

As he arrived, a huge ring of people pressed around the front of the Club. Smoke was coming out of windows and the

51

holes in the top which had been broken open by the fire department. Firemen, policemen, doctors, undertakers, volunteers, and fortune seekers worked feverishly. Those who were obviously dead were carted off to the mortuary; others were given medical assistance. It was difficult to hold back the crowd.

Raymond first walked up to three sisters who were unable to find their missing sister. These were some of the most beautiful girls in Natchez, with their olive brown complexions, long black hair, and heavy eyelashes. The two older sisters were in Raymond's class and were Jean's best friends. As Raymond saw them, he threw his bandaged hands around their necks and cried, "Thank God, you're safe." In the same breath he asked, "Where is Jean? Is she safe?"

The oldest sister answered, "Yes, someone told me he saw her but I haven't. Are you burned badly?"

"Not so bad," said Raymond. "I'd feel like a million if I could only know she is all right."

"Our young sister is still missing. If you see her, tell her we're all right."

"Okay," said Raymond, as he continued his search.

It was then nearly three o'clock in the morning. Many of the bodies had been carried away, and the police and deputized assistants were on hand to prevent unauthorized persons from entering the charred dance hall. Every precaution was being taken to prevent the taking of money and jewelry from the dead. Walking around in the vicinity of the Rhythm Club where the tense and anxious crowd was still gathered, Raymond met Frank Renfro, an old school chum who lived in Natchez.

"Boy, you are really burned. Better let me get you to a doctor."

"No, no, Frank," replied Raymond. "I'm not so bad off as I look. I think I could forget all these burns if only I could find Jean. I know Mr. and Mrs. Gravier are worried to death."

Frank was quiet for a moment. Knowing how deeply attached Raymond was to Jean, he felt inadequate to the task which confronted him. Mustering his courage, he said, "Ray, I guess I just as well tell you as anyone—they say Jean was lost."

"No, no, you're lying. She couldn't be." Raymond exploded. This outburst turned immediately into tears when he realized that it could be true.

"How do you know? I was just told she was alive."

"Jimmy Richards said he saw them taking her away. But don't take my word. Let's go to every funeral home and make a check. Do you feel like it?"

"Yes. Let's go. I just couldn't go back until I find her. Please, God," he cried, "don't let this be true. Please."

Frank, knowing the location of the undertaker's parlors, led the search. In an effort to take Raymond's mind off Jean, he began telling how he escaped. "I was sitting at a table in the back of the hall when the crowd came rushing toward me. I jumped under the table. I clutched both legs in my hands to make sure that no one would knock it from over me. The lights went out and I could see the door through the fire and smoke. I pulled out my handkerchief and started spitting on it. I spat over and over on it, then I put it over my face and started toward the door. The coast was clear and with this handkerchief over my face I simply got my hair singed and a little burn on my ear. You can bet I was glad to see that door."

Raymond had not interrupted Frank as he talked. Then he said dryly, "In a case like that, I could think of a quicker way to wet a handkerchief."

By that time, they had reached the Century Undertaking Company, the smallest in the city. They searched with great anxiety but, happily for them, Jean was not there. From there to the Bluff City Undertaking Company, the largest, but Jean was not among its dead. If only she isn't at the National Undertaking Company, then she is alive, thought Raymond. When they reached this last mortuary, Raymond entered fearfully. As he stepped in the door, he saw a woman sitting, gazing stoically at two daughters lying still on the floor. As Frank made his way through the funeral home, the bereaved mother intoned: "I begged them not to go—not to go. They'd be alive today if they had just listened to their poor old ignorant mother. Lord, have mercy on their souls."

Frank had walked about midway across the floor and had bent over as if to make an identification. He soon straightened up and beckoned for Raymond, who approached with slow uncertainty. When Raymond was a few paces away, Frank said, "Ray, brace yourself for a shock."

Raymond knew then that Jean was dead. He walked up and supported himself on Frank's shoulder. He looked down and there she was—lifeless, among others who had shared her fate. As if he expected a response, he stooped down, placed his hands on both sides of her head and gazed at her unseared face. It was obvious that she had suffocated. Her pretty face was tarnished with smut and dirt, a small part of her long auburn hair was burned, and a small, one-inch blister was on the right side of her chin. As Raymond stood up, it appeared that he would take the blow with the same calm serenity and determination as the mother at the door. Suddenly, he felt as if his very breath were being choked off, as if he, too, were suffocating. He fell unconscious to the floor.

Frank placed his hands under Raymond's forearms and dragged him to the front of the room. Another man helped Frank carry Raymond to a car and drove a few blocks to a doctor's office. They found the office crowded with hysterical patients. Ordinarily, it would have taken Raymond hours to see the doctor. But since he had passed out and the others waiting thought him to be dead, they were willing to yield their turns to him. In this way he was taken quickly into the doctor's office. After reviving Raymond, the doctor looked at his burns. Noticing the castor oil and soda on his hands, he inquired, "How did you get all of this stuff on you?"

Raymond replied, "An old white lady down the street put it on me. I got weak and passed out in front of her house and she gave me first aid. Is it bad?"

"No," answered the doctor. "You're in pretty good shape— much better shape than many of those people in the outer office. However, I'll treat you since you are in here." So he cut off with scissors what was left of Raymond's messy shirt.

The doctor and his assistant removed the homemade bandages, cleaned the burns, covered the seared surface with a tannic acid solution, and gave Raymond an anesthetic. Learning that Raymond was from Sweethill, he advised him to hurry back to the campus and "report to my good friend, Dr. Sims." "Tell him I sent my regards and how much we need his service out here. So long, son." He tapped Raymond on the backside. "You'll be all right in a little while." Frank took off his shirt, split the sleeves and carefully draped it around Raymond's bandage-covered body.

Raymond paused and said "Thank you, doc. Guess that's all the pay I can give you now, but I'll send it to you."

Doc smiled. "Don't worry about that, son; you'll repay me well by getting well. Good night."

"Good night, doc," replied Frank and Raymond in unison as Frank closed the office door. The outer office was still crowded and periodic cries went up from would-be patients who were suffering from shock or the intensity of their burns. Although he felt better at that moment, he could sympathize with the others who were awaiting treatment. His heart was heavy for them as he departed from the office.

The car and the driver who brought them to the doctor's office were nowhere to be found, so they had to walk back to where their car was parked. Frank took the shortcuts and supported Raymond on his shoulder. Raymond kept assuring Frank that he could walk under his own power, but Frank refused to take a chance of Raymond's collapsing again. As they reached the vicinity of the dance hall, they heard screaming. On St. Catherine Street, they saw thousands of people still milling around, hoping that their loved ones would, through some miracle, be found alive. Raymond paused for a moment as he passed the front of the charred hall, but resumed his pace when Frank gave him a slight pull. "Frank," he said, "the memories of that place will haunt me the rest of my life. I hope I never see the inside of a dance hall again."

They walked on in silence until they reached the car. Two of his college buddies were waiting. As Raymond and Frank looked around, they noticed that Oliver Hasty was missing. "Where is Oliver?" asked Raymond, to divert attention from himself.

"I don't know," replied John Turrin, the driver. "After I see that you are all right, I'll go and search for him. Just what happened to you, Raymond? Tell me about it."

As Raymond was about to relate his experiences, Frank interceded. "Don't make him talk about it now. He's burned pretty badly and doesn't feel well. He'll tell you later."

They helped Raymond into the back seat of the car. After that, John told the others that he was going to search for Oliver. Before he left, Frank informed him of Jean's death. "My God!" he exclaimed, and walked quickly away.

John was gone for approximately fifteen minutes. Returning to the car, he announced in a trembling voice, "Boys, Oliver won't be riding back with us tonight or ever. He's dead." He began to weep. "I knew he was dead when I left a few minutes ago, but I just couldn't bring myself to face it. I had seen him, fellows. I knew I just had to go back again. I kept saying to myself, 'It can't be true; it can't be true,' though all the time I knew it was." The others wept unashamedly. Raymond, who himself had flirted with death and had seen the life of his sweetheart snuffed out, joined the boys and wept openly for Jean, for his friends, and for the pains which pierced his flesh as well as his heart.

Four-thirty Wednesday morning found them still in the city of Natchez. A degree of calmness had come to the car. One by one, they were beginning to realize that the old gang had been broken up. Oliver Hasty was an irreplaceable missing link. This strange destiny had to be faced. "Let's go, boys," said John Turrin as he cranked the car and pulled off. The streets were crowded still. Fog from the river and smoke from the dance hall combined with the smell of burnt flesh hung heavily over the streets.

As the car cruised along at a moderate speed, a morbid silence settled over the group. The day was breaking and they all wanted to get back to the dormitory before the students began to stir. They could not risk speeding—it would just be their luck to have an accident. The miles seemed longer than ever. Although it was only thirty-eight miles, it was exactly six-thirty when they arrived on campus. They hurried to their respective rooms to avoid the crowd. However, they knew that news of the Natchez fire would soon come to light. Raymond needed to be hospitalized upon arrival, and the news of the deaths of Jean and Oliver certainly could not long be kept secret. The boys knew that they had to report to school authorities, but there were certain details that they pledged never to tell.

Sweethill imposed strict regulations upon both its male and female students. Young men at the freshmen and sophomore levels were required to undergo a bed check. In order to make it appear that someone was in the bed, they had rolled up blankets and pillows under the spread and pulled the spread over the human-like form. Consequently, each boy had successfully passed the curfew inspection. While they knew that this little scheme would be uncovered, there was one that had to remain a secret—the mode of transportation.

Teacher-student fraternization was perhaps one of the least pardonable sins on the campus. Yet a certain young male teacher welcomed the opportunity to join the boys in bull sessions and would occasionally use his newly purchased car to carry them to dances in nearby cities. That night he was to take the five boys to Natchez, but, unexpectedly, the dean called a meeting. The teacher, rather than disappoint the boys, agreed to let them have the car after obtaining pledges of secrecy. He must have had a premonition of the impending danger for he even made the driver promise to say that he had stolen the car in the event of a wreck. Out of respect for this teacher, the boys reaffirmed their pledges that no one would ever make them divulge this secret.

Arriving on campus, they drove the car to its usual parking place. The young teacher was standing in the doorway. A quick explanation was given and the boys hastened out of sight. Two of Raymond's buddies escorted him to the hospital, which was about two hundred yards from Raymond's building. Raymond's face, neck, hands, and shoulders were seared and blistered and he was beginning to suffer excruciating pain. As he reached the white frame three-story building, fear began to seize him.

"Don't worry, Raymond," said his buddies as one pressed the doorbell.

"You fellows are worried about me, but you better think about yourselves. You can see that I'll never be able to return to school, but you fellows will be kicked out. I just hope to heaven the `ole man' has a heart and lets you stay."

"Just go on, buddy, and get well. We're prepared to take things in stride. Best of everything to you, boy, and we'll see you." One friend left and Frank remained.

A pretty brown-skinned student nurse named Ida Anderson answered the door. Raymond would have preferred having anyone except her answer the door. He knew her too well and had a guilt complex where she was concerned. On one weekend when Jean went home, he had taken Ida to the movie on Friday night and the dance on Saturday night. He had kissed her and told her he loved her. She had questioned him and accused him of being "color struck," but he assured her that he preferred brown-skinned girls any day.

Ida was certainly a petite, charming brown-skinned doll. Her father was a well-to-do insurance man who could afford to dress her in the latest fashions. On Sundays, she would come out dressed like a queen in gowns that would emphasize all her curves. The boys, watching her pass, would praise her figure among themselves by saying that she was "built like a brick outhouse" or "shaped like a Coca-Cola bottle." She carried herself with poise and self-assurance and had many suitors, but never allowed herself to become serious with any. Raymond had been most surprised when she had agreed to go to the movie with him and greatly disturbed when he detected that she was falling for him. He wished he could be two men so he could deserve the love of both Jean and Ida. He had to make a choice and he knew that choice was Jean. Not being man enough to tell Ida of his decision, he had avoided meeting her face to face. She had helped Raymond in this matter by not seeking to exact an explanation from him.

Seeing Ida's compassionate face, Raymond knew that he would have to depend on her to nurse him back to health. Not only would he have to explain the causes of his physical ailments, but he would certainly feel an obligation to explain his actions after their romantic weekend.

Without showing any emotional disturbance, she said "Come on in, Raymond. You been hurt, haven't you? Burned?"

"Yes," replied Raymond.

Frank, who was still standing at the door, said, "Ray, you're in good hands now, so I'm leaving. You'll see me later on today. Take care of him, Ida. I must get back to the dormitory."

Turning to Raymond, she asked, "Are you in pain?"

"Yes. But not like I was an hour or so ago. Guess I'm all doped up right now."

Ida eased her arm gently around his waist and with her other hand, she placed his bandaged hand across her shoulders. "We have a nice private room on the third floor and since the doctor isn't in, I'll take the liberty of putting you in there.

You know I want only the best for you. Just lean on me and I will give you all the support you need." Raymond knew that he really did not need physical support at that time, but he could not rob Ida of the feeling that she was helping him when he needed it most.

Reaching the third floor, Ida led Raymond into the private room, then called the registered nurse to report the incoming patient. The R.N. instructed Ida to get him a pair of pajamas, put him to bed, and to put unguentine and gauze on the burned spots as a temporary precaution. Ida answered affirmatively, forgetting that her patient, with both hands bandaged, would be unable to dress himself. She then realized the embarrassment that this would cause to both Ray and herself, yet she knew it had to be done. First, she pulled off Raymond's shoes and socks. "I'll have to put some pajamas on you."

"I'm not that helpless," replied Raymond. "Just give them to me and I'll be able to put them on."

Raymond's hands were swollen tightly and it was obvious that he could not even hold his pajamas, much less put them on. Ida took a pair of scissors and cut off the sleeves of his shirt, then unbuttoned it gently and pulled it off. Ida covered the blistered part heavily with unguentine and bandaged it with gauze. Then she put on the top part of his pajamas. Trying to sound like a professional, she said "Young man, I'm your nurse, and I'll put pajamas on you this morning if it's the last thing I do. If you cooperate, there'll be no embarrassment."

She then made Raymond lie back on the bed. She spread a sheet over him and pushed it up under his arms. "You hold the sheet and I'll pull your pants and underwear off, and then I'll put on the pajama pants."

"Yes, ma'am, Nurse," Raymond said, forcing a smile.

Ida performed her task skillfully. "There," she said. "You are properly dressed. I told you that I would take care of you, and I mean it. Just remember, no task is too difficult for me to perform—especially when I'm taking care of you. I'm your nurse, whether you want it or not, and I'll see that you have the very best of care—the best of care. Go to sleep and get some rest. I don't have a class until one o'clock. I'll call the doctor, now, but don't worry. I'll be here if you need me." Lightly, she stroked him on the chest and repeated, "Go to sleep now."

Raymond slept for nearly two hours. At eight-thirty, Ida came in and found him awake.

"Good morning," she said pleasantly.

"Good morning," replied Raymond.

"Want some breakfast?" asked Ida. "Have some for you right here."

"Thank you," responded Raymond, "but you'll have to feed me. I'm helpless as a baby."

Without commenting, Ida sat down on the side of the bed and began feeding him gently. Raymond observed through eyes stinging with the effect of fire not just a beautiful girl, but a big-hearted girl.

"Now then, young man," she said when he had finished. "You have had a good breakfast and if you feel like it, I want you to tell me about your burns. You've told me you were trapped in a fire in Natchez, but otherwise you've been mum on everything. Can you tell me about it now?"

"You're sweet," said Ray. "Yes, I guess I should have told you the whole story voluntarily. It's one of those things you'd like to forget but couldn't in a million years." Then step by step, he told of his experience, the death of Jean, the deaths of

Hasty and of hundreds of others. Ida was astonished. She opened her mouth, then suddenly covered it with her hand. "Oh my gosh," she exclaimed. "Oh my gosh, Ray, I am truly sorry to hear that—truly sorry. It doesn't seem that God would suffer that to be true. I can see why you didn't want to talk. Yet, you know it's best to. It relieves that pent-up feeling."

Ida looked at her watch and noticed that it was a few minutes before nine. "Gee," she said, "it's just about nine and Doctor Sims will be in any minute now. Let me tidy your bed up a bit." Pausing for a minute, she snapped her fingers and with her winning little smile, she asked, "Wanta bet? Bet you old Doc will say, "I remember when I had a patient like you back in Nashville—only he was much worse off."

"No," replied Raymond with a faint smile. "I know I'd lose." Although Doc had finished at Meharry Medical College and been a general practitioner in Mississippi most of his professional life, everyone on the campus knew that he'd been everywhere, done everything, and what he did not know in the field of medicine just was not worth knowing.

"You are wise to him, I see. Yet, with all that conceit—with that defensive facade, he's still a pretty good doctor. I must carry your tray back to the kitchen. I'll be back later."

As Ida left his room, he began thinking about old Doc Sims. He smiled to himself as he recalled Doc's account of how his effective medical practice saved three lives at the same time— a white woman's, her baby's and his. According to the story, Doc was returning home from his evening round. As he pulled up in front of his house, he saw two white men sitting in a pickup truck. One got out and approached his car and with an uncultured southern drawl asked, "Ain't you that colored doctor they told me about?"

Doc answered, "I'm colored and I'm the doctor here at the College."

"Well, it's you I want to see. The old Missus is sick—sick bad and needs a doctor."

Doc Sims replied, "You don't want me, you were probably looking for the white doctor. He lives about four miles up the road."

"Him," said the white stranger, "I wouldn't let him treat my dog," pointing to an old spotted hound in the back of the truck. "I come after you, Doc, and you gotta go, you gotta go, Doc, cause the old Missus needs you bad. Get in, Doc, cause we gotta hurry."

"Who are you?" inquired Doc Sims.

"Joe Redhead. And if you're a doctor, no harm will come to you."

By that time, Mrs. Sims had come to the door and Dr. Sims gave her this explanation. "Mr. Redhead has cattle sick and wants me to look at them. Of course, I'm not a veterinarian, but if it makes him feel better I'll go out."

"Do be careful," responded Mrs. Sims. "You know his reputation."

"Don't worry, honey. I'll be back when I get back."

As Doc approached the truck, his mind ran briefly over the Redheads' reputation. They were a family with a large group of boys who had secured about two thousand acres of bottom land near the Mississippi River. They had many blacks living on that plantation who were virtually peons. When they let their black tenants come into the little town on Saturday evening, they would raise cain! Nobody wanted to tangle with "them Redhead Niggers" for to tangle with them was to tangle with the Redhead boys, and they were known to kill "uppity niggers." Rumor had it that a black man lost a cow and heard that it had gotten in with the Redhead herd. Knowing that he could identify his cow by his brand, he bravely went over and requested permission to look over the herd. Unfortunately, neither the black man nor the cow had been seen since this bold venture. Doc knew well the Redheads' reputation and he was mindful of this as he left.

En route to the plantation, Redhead began to explain the nature of the old Missus' illness. "You see," he said, "she's having a baby—the ninth it is. She's having some trouble. Been having it for two days. I got a nigger midwife out there, but she don't know nothing. So I come for you 'cause she said you've been to school and know everything. Until this chap come along, me and my wife had eight head. Auntie Martha, as good a nigger midwife as God ever made, brought all of 'em here and never lost a one. Auntie Sarah, the nigger who's with her now, don't know a damn thing. So, Doc, we come for you 'cause you know everything."

Suppose she dies, he thought. Since the woman had been in labor so long, Doc knew he was taking the case at a disadvantage. He must keep her alive because his staying alive was dependent upon her staying alive.

Farmer Redhead drove at a breakneck speed. Doc felt that his life was in double jeopardy—death from a possible wreck or death at the hands of Joe Redhead. The first crisis was overcome when the truck pulled up in front of the spacious plantation house. Not the old antebellum mansion, but a large simple dwelling with a screen-enclosed front porch. Crisis made the Redheads forget southern social etiquette, and the doctor was invited to enter through the front door.

As Doc reached the bedroom, he saw a pale, pain-stricken white woman lying in an antique bed. As he entered, Auntie

Sarah, the midwife, stood up and greeted him. Before he could return the greeting, the white woman called faintly, "Doctor, please help me." In the woman's words as well as in the behavior of Joe Redhead, Doc said he could see a changing South, a place where traditionalism, superstition, and segregation would inevitably fail in times of crisis when confronted by education, reason and rationalism. Doc observed the numerous superstitious practices in which so much faith had been placed. Tied across from post to post of the bed was a sheet. This sheet had been used to pull up on to aid in labor. There was also a derby hat on the table. This was used to blow in when labor pains came. This was calculated to hasten the process of delivery. Underneath the bed was an old rusty ax which was supposed to cut the pains. Jestingly, Doc said to his class, "Any fool should have had sense enough to use a razor rather than an ax." More remarkable than the yielding of superstition to sound medical practice was the yielding of a southern taboo—having a black man do obstetrical work on a white woman. (Yet, the choice between life and death made the Redheads forget the taboo and place the white "ole Missus" in the hands of a black man.)

Doc recalled that as he entered the house, he saw a gun rack and several guns near the door. While conscious of their presence and the inclination of Redhead to use them, he felt that he must have acceptable conditions under which to work. Mustering his courage, he turned to Redhead and a white woman visitor and said, "I must ask and insist that everyone leave the room except Auntie Sarah. We can work better like that and we'll keep you informed on how she's getting along." To the white visitor, he gave this order: "You can help us by keeping hot water ready." Redhead and the visitor complied but not before Redhead reassured the doctor with these words:

"Doc, we counting on you to save ole Missus. Just save her, Doc, and nothing is going to happen to you."

Doc and Auntie Sarah spent many anxious hours with the laboring woman, occasionally assuring Redhead and the family that all was progressing as favorably as could be expected. The "ole Missus," while in pain, seemed relieved as he assured her that all was going to be well. Doc's anxiety ended about midnight, when an eight and one-half pound boy was born, normal in every respect. His dedication to save life had led him to bring into the world a child destined to be indoctrinated in a land of "segregation, sowbelly, and sorghum," a white child who would probably learn to oppress and exploit—Joe Redhead-style.

Doc Sims called Farmer Redhead in along with the visitor and showed them the baby. He assured him that the mother would be all right, but needed rest. Then, Redhead gave him this compliment: "Auntie Sarah was right. You're the best nigger doctor this side of the Mississippi. We can never thank you enough." Redhead gave Doc twenty-five dollars and two large hams, and returned him to his home at four-thirty in the morning. Doctor Sims was to make several professional trips to the Redheads' home, and the family became some of his best patients.

Doctor Sims walked into Raymond's room shortly after nine. His lab coat was draped neatly around a well-fitted collar and tie. His hair was brushed back neatly from his brown face and a streak of gray gave him a most distinguished look. With a broad smile which showed a perfect set of pearly white teeth, he asked: "How's my young man this morning?"

Raymond answered, "All right, doctor." Then he thought and said, "Well, maybe I'm not all right."

At that instant, Doc cut in and said: "Maybe the flesh is a little frail at this moment, but, son, I can see that the spirit is strong. If you keep that spirit up, I'll have you out of here sooner than you think." Then he began, "When I was back in Nashville, son, I had a patient who was three times as old as you and burned three times as bad. Now wait, let me examine you." As he examined, he continued. "She was burned from head to foot, but I put her back almost in perfect condition. I even had to do a little skin grafting, and you could hardly tell she'd been scarred. At your age and with these being practically superficial burns, I'll make you as good as new."

"But doctor, will my face be white?" asked Raymond.

"Yes, for a while, but unguentine and sunlight will restore your handsome Indian color. Your hair has been burned—it might not come back as thick as before. Don't worry, young man," Doc boasted, "You have two things in your favor—youth and a good doctor."

"Thank you, doctor," said Raymond. Doc left as he assured Raymond that he would see him later in the day. During the thirty-three days that were to follow, Raymond spent his days under the professional care of Doctor Sims, the registered nurse and the loving care of Ida.

Chapter IV

When Raymond learned that his burns were serious enough to keep him hospitalized for several weeks, he realized he had to break the sad news to his parents. This was the most difficult task he had ever faced because he had to confess that he had violated the religious and moral codes of his home training. Truly, he was a prodigal son. He was not at all sure that his father would have compassion. His father and mother struggled to send him off to college to get an education, placing him among the select few who were to become the diploma elite in Mississippi. The height of ungratefulness was to squander this opportunity. In search of a good time, or as his father would say, in search of the flesh, he had thrown away his chance. It was not the personal loss that disturbed him, but the heartbreak that he had brought to his parents. To him, the most bitter fruit of sin was the pain of confession.

Raymond's feeling of guilt was proportionate to his reckoning of the disgrace he had brought on his family. His father was an upstanding man in his community, a prosperous farmer, and a steward in the Methodist Church—Chairman of the Steward Board. Everyone respected him as in industrious Christian man who tried to bring up his family in the fear and admonition of God. When he elected to send his sons to college, both white and black citizens labeled him a fool. "Pat, you're a fool to work your fingers to the bone to keep your kids in school. They'll never be any help to you. Once they get educated, they'll turn their sophisticated noses up at all you ever stood for. If you would realize that college is for white folk, you could take your boys and turn out one of the best cotton crops in southwestern Mississippi." Raymond's father had withstood this pessimistic advice and had gambled on giving his boys a better chance than he had been given. He wanted to give them something that no white man could take away—a good education. Raymond had betrayed his trust. He made his father a fool in the eyes of his peers. Having wrecked his father's dream, Raymond decided that he could retain at least some honor by telling his father about the disaster that had befallen him.

Upon Ida's return from class, he called her to his bedside. "Ida," he said, "I want you to do something for me right away, please. Will you?"

"Yes, Ray," said Ida with a smile and a wink of the eye. "You name it and I'll deliver it, pronto."

"Ida," said Ray, "I want you to call my parents and tell them about my accident. Break it to them gently and don't tell them that it's serious. Tell them that I'll be in the hospital a couple of days, but just for observation. You know how to fix it up. The milder you make it, the better."

"Okay, Raymond, but where do I call?" said Ida.

Raymond remembered that his family could not be reached by phone. As a matter of fact, in his hometown there was only one phone on the black side of the track—at the colored funeral home. All incoming calls for blacks went there and the mortician would have his messenger take them to the proper person. Each person was expected to pay a small fee for this service. He advised Ida to call the funeral home and ask them to take the message out to the farm immediately.

Ida made her way to the first phone booth and, with her own money, placed a call to the colored funeral home. She explained the situation to the mortician and prevailed upon him not to make the accident sound serious. He assured her that he was experienced in delivering bad news and creating only a minimum amount of excitement.

Unfortunately, the mortician could not deliver the message in person—he got one of the boys to deliver it for him. The kindly mortician urged the boy not to exaggerate when he broke the news. Lacking the necessary tact, however, the inexperienced messenger carried a message of near fatality. Arriving at the farm, he found Mrs. Miles out in the field looking over the new cotton crop. A robust woman with long plaits hanging carelessly from underneath her wide straw hat, she greeted him with a smile.

"What brings you out this way?" she asked.

"I got some bad news for you," he answered. "Someone just called from Sweethill and said that your boy Raymond was burned up in a dance hall in Natchez last night."

"No, heavens, no," sobbed Mrs. Miles. "My baby boy can't be dead. It can't be true. He was in Sweethill, not in Natchez."

Realizing his mistake, the messenger broke in, "Mrs. Miles, Mrs. Miles, Raymond ain't dead, he's just in the hospital. It's true because someone just called us a few minutes ago."

Mrs. Miles quieted down and said to the messenger, "You just wait right here because I want you to take me to the mill where my husband works. Wait just a few minutes and I'll be ready." Then she went into the house to dress while the messenger waited in the car.

In the meantime, Pat Miles, who was working at the mill nine miles away, had heard the story and at that moment was en route home to tell his wife. About eleven o'clock, "Little Pat," as he was called by the mill hands, had been making one of his regular trips up the ramp when Buster Jackson, a burly black man known for his ability to lie, called to him and said, "I know your baby boy wouldn't want me to tell you this, but I saw him at the dance in Natchez last night. The dance hall caught on fire about midnight and about half of the niggers in it were roasted. Something tells me that your boy was burned up with that group."

Pat laughed. "Buster, you're a liar. In the first place, my boy can't dance. In the second place, he's in school and can't get out at night. I'd almost be willing to bet my bottom dollar that you were right over in the quarters sound asleep yourself."

Buster tried to sound convincing. "Little Pat, you know I make all dances where they are likely to have good-looking broads, and boy, they have nothing but high yellows over there. Anytime I hear of something like that, you know I'm gone. That's all I work for. So please believe me, Little Pat, I'm telling the truth this time. Cross my heart and hope to die in my tracks. I know I saw your boy there last night."

Pat picked up his cart and started down the ramp. He looked back over his shoulder and yelled, "Buster, if lying were dollars, you'd be a millionaire."

Although Pat knew Buster's reputation for lying, when the lie happens to be about one's family, it cannot be dismissed easily. So, the words of Buster crept into his mind—"I know I saw your boy there last night . . . something tells me he was burned up with that group." Pat, betting on the training that he had given his boy, assured himself that his boy could not have been there—even if there had been a dance and a fire. He did not assign any credibility to Buster's tale until about twelve forty-five during the lunch hour when the straw boss walked up to his group and said, "I just heard on the news that about 200 'Nigras' were burned up in a dance hall last night."

Pat jumped up and started toward the office. Maybe Buster wasn't lying, he thought. Maybe my boy was in there. When he arrived at the office, he walked in and spoke to the boss.

"Howdy, Mr. Seaborn. I want to call Sweethill college. Buster Jackson said he saw my boy at the dance last night where all those people were burned to death. So, Mr. Seaborn, I just gotta check."

"Do you know how to call, Pat?" asked Mr. Seaborn.

"No, sir," he replied. "I'll like for you to do it for me. Just call the college and ask the president is my boy, Raymond Miles, all right?"

In a matter of minutes, Mr. Seaborn had the president on the phone, who confirmed that Raymond had attended the dance and had been burned. Mr. Seaborn turned to Pat and said, "Your boy was there all right, but he's back at school in the hospital. Doing all right, so that president said."

"Thank you, Mr. Seaborn," said Pat. "But I must ask you another favor. I want this evening off because I plan to be in Sweethill before dark."

"Go on, Pat. If you need any money or any help, let me know."

"Thank you, Mr. Seaborn; I'll be back when I can."

As Pat was leaving the plant, he met Buster Jackson. Before Buster could speak, Pat offered his apologies. "I just couldn't believe you, Buster, but my boy was there. He wasn't burned to death, but he's in the hospital at Sweethill. Thank you for telling me."

"I can't blame you for not believing me. You know, I lie and cut the fool so much until I don't believe the truth when I tell it myself. Hope he's all right."

"Thank you," said Pat. Buster headed back to his job and Pat got his car and headed home to pick up his wife.

At his home, he found the messenger waiting to carry Mother Miles to the mill. Mr. Miles gave him a quarter and thanked him for bringing out the message.

"Dear, how can you explain it?" said Papa Miles. "We try so hard to set the right example and instill in those boys sound Christian principles; yet, no sooner do they get away, than they are led astray. Where did we fail? I just can't wait to give him a piece of my mind."

"Don't get upset, sweetheart. Boys will be boys. While they might stray temporarily, they will eventually return to old home training. So you're not going up there and give him a piece of your mind. If I know that boy, he is worried to death and eating his heart out for having made this mistake. Let's pray to God that his burns are not serious and that the president will let him stay in school. His own conscience will punish him enough. We'll not argue with him. What he needs most now is love and affection and that we'll give him."

"Okay, Mama," said Papa Miles. "You always did have a way with that boy. I'll be quiet and let you handle it."

As they set out for Sweethill, Papa Miles said, "I hope this old car doesn't fail us today. If not, we should be in Sweethill in two and a half hours." Both parents were filled with deep anxiety for their son. Most of the trip was spent in silence. Perhaps both were praying silently for their son who had strayed.

Back at Sweethill, Ida informed Raymond that she had delivered the message to the funeral home. He thanked Ida and told her that he expected his parents before sundown.

That afternoon, Raymond's roommate Frank brought his toiletry articles to the hospital and gave them to Ida. He wanted to come up and see Raymond, but the doctor ordered that he was to see no one. Doc Sims had realized that when this news struck the campus, curiosity seekers would have been rushing to see Ray, in addition to his many friends.

Ida sat down on the side of the bed and gently combed the back section of the hair that had not been burned. She gently applied the medication and told him about the numerous friends who had asked about him. She told him that while he could not expect any student visitors, he was certain to have a special visitor after four—the president of the college. Raymond knew that the discipline committee usually got credit for handling infractions of college rules, but everybody knew that the president exercised the final judgment on such matters. So this evening would unquestionably determine whether he stayed in school or not. He felt as helpless as a wayward Spaniard coming before the Inquisition. The punishment was left to be meted out. Surely, the president would want to know whose car was used. The friends had agreed that they would say one of the student's cars was used and Raymond would stick by that pledge.

The hour spent in waiting was complete torture. Why not have him come in and expel me outright, he thought. The college president was admired by both teachers and students for his apparent brilliance. The fact that he was trained in psychology led students to believe that it was useless to lie to him. They used to say, "You just as well come clean with `Pres'. It's no use trying to `psych' him because he can see right through you." Realizing that he could not outwit the president, Raymond made up his mind to agree to withdraw without questions if the president thought it best.

The president, a tall, nattily dressed man, entered Raymond's room at exactly 4:00 p.m., looked down on Raymond, smiled, and said in a gentle manner, "How are you feeling, son?"

"All right, sir. I don't feel any physical pain at this time, but my heart is aching for the number of people that I've hurt—let down."

"I understand, son. Don't worry; the doctor said you'll be all right and should be able to return to classes within two weeks."

"You mean I won't be kicked out of school?"

"While I would agree that you should be expelled, if Jesus had compassion, why shouldn't we? I am recommending that all of you boys be given eleven demerits with the understanding that one more this session will mean automatic expulsion. Somehow, I feel that you boys have suffered enough and will suffer a great deal in the future. There's only one thing—how did you make the trip down to Natchez?"

"We went in Jim's station wagon," said Raymond.

"Good. All you boys said the same thing. I just wanted to make sure that none of my teachers were mixed up in this with my students. Best wishes, son," he said, and departed.

As he left, Raymond knew that the president had seen through their lie. He knew that someone on the faculty had given them aid. While he would always believe this, the boys would never confirm his belief.

After the five-thirty meal, Raymond leaned back on his raised bed for a moment of meditation. In the midst of all of his trouble, he thought how fortunate he was to have such an understanding nurse as Ida. Not only was she efficient in her work, but she fully understood and commiserated with his plight. She had all those qualities that would make a man who was ready to die want to live.

About six o'clock, Ida rushed in with a broad smile. "Brace yourself, Raymond, because if I'm seeing correctly, the Miles chiefs are coming in."

Ida straightened the spread, fastened Raymond's collar and tried to bolster his spirits to meet his irate parents. As she heard their footsteps on the stairs, Ida stepped over to the distant corner and stood smiling, trying to give Raymond moral support. The nurse walked in and said gently, "You have company." Mama, Papa and Emmit walked in.

"Hello, baby," Mama said, as she fought to hold back the tears. "We got your call and we came as soon as we could."

"Hi, Mama, Papa, Emmit. I'm glad you came. I guess I look bad, but the doctor said I'm doing all right."

By that time, Papa Miles had stepped near the bed. "Where else are you burned, son?" he asked, as he looked down on the seared face and neck of his son.

Without answering, Raymond pulled both of his bandaged hands from under the sheet. Seeing them, Mama Miles could no longer hold back the tears. She broke down and sobbed loudly. "Oh! My poor boy, my baby boy. Why did God let this happen to him?" Raymond quickly turned his head to the wall and made every effort to control his emotions. As hard as he tried, he found himself unable to do so—he, too, was overcome and wept unashamedly.

Ida stood in the corner watching this emotional display. Nothing would have suited her better at that moment than to join Mama Miles and Raymond in a good cry. She told herself that such behavior would never do for a nurse. Being a nurse trainee, she restrained her feelings and walked over to Mother Miles and led her gently out of the room into the hallway. There, Ida whispered softly to her.

"Mrs. Miles, Mrs. Miles," said Ida, in a soft but firm tone, "Please get a hold on yourself. I know how you must feel, but you can't allow Raymond to see you go to pieces like that again. He's been awfully depressed all day. He is almost overwhelmed by the burden that he must carry in his heart. I know you love him. But, right now, love for him can be shown best through your strength. He needs your strength far more than he needs your pity. So get yourself together quickly and go back in there and give him what he needs to get up and back in school. I'm not a psychiatrist, but it's my guess that Raymond could profit more from empathy and understanding than he could from the medical treatment administered by ole Doc Sims."

"I'm sorry," replied Mother Miles. I'm ready to go back now and I promise I won't allow myself to fall apart again."

As Mrs. Miles was uttering these words, she was also firmly drying her tears. She then entered the room where Raymond and Papa Miles were beginning to talk. Mrs. Miles showed remarkable composure and pulled up to the bedside as Raymond started relating his story.

Raymond described the dance hall, its decoration, and its one exit. He did not blame the manager of the Rhythm Night Club for having inadequate exits as much as he blamed the irrational behavior of the dancers. As he saw it, many lives were unnecessarily lost because people lost the power to think in the face of a crisis. "I'm not saying that I'm brave, Mama, because you know I'm not. You would be the first to know that I was scared of going in a dark room at my own house until I was fourteen. Yet, it was my ability to reason—to remain calm in the face of danger—that helped me stay alive.

"If I didn't know how much my dying under those circumstances would have hurt you, I could say now that I wish I were not alive. Now don't stop me because I'm not crazy. I'm saying what I feel and mean. Mama, you and Papa have heard me speak of Jean Gravier."

"Yes," said Mother and Papa Miles in unison. "Well," Raymond continued, "She lost her life because of me. I insisted on her going to the dance and she didn't escape. Really, I did all I could to help her, but I failed. I know my soul could rest better if I had died trying to save her."

"Don't blame yourself," said Mama Miles. "The paper said over 200 lost their lives. When you know that you have done all you can do, angels in heaven can do no more."

Just then, they heard Dr. Sims' voice in the hallway. Raymond knew that his parents would leave. "Mama, I want you and Papa to do something for me. I want you to go through Natchez and go to the Graviers' home, and tell them how sorry I am. Tell them this just as I'm saying it to you—that I wish it were possible for me to join Jean wherever she may be. I also want you to find out when her funeral will be held and represent me. Try to make friends with the Graviers because they are some of the best people God ever made. Also, take my sister with you to the funeral and ask her to use her shorthand skills and take down every word that is said."

"All right, son. You can count on us. Don't blame yourself for what happened. God moves in a mysterious way. This may have been his way of testing the faith of his children. At a time like this, you can find strength in the trials and tribulations of Job. You remember how God allowed the devil to destroy all that he had, and how Job's wife asked him to curse God and die. What did Job say? `Though he slay me, I will trust him.' So, boy, you have a lot to live for. God has placed this test on you. Try to have the faith of a Job. God could have taken you, but he left you here because he had a purpose for you to fulfill. Whatever you do, keep faith in Him."

As Providence would have it, Doc Sims entered before Raymond could reply. Had he made this reply, his words would have certainly tormented Papa and Mama Miles, because he was ready to admit that his faith in the Almighty had been shaken. That night of agony in Natchez had made him see a God of wrath rather than a God of love and mercy. It had made him come to grips with the age-old question of why the good suffer.

If Raymond had had time to express his thoughts, he would have shocked Mama and Papa Miles by saying that it is extremely difficult to have faith in a God who kills and inflicts human suffering indiscriminately. Raymond would have identified as good people those who were apparently the standard bearers of morality in their community. People who by the lives they lived were dedicated to evangelistic service for their Creator and his coming Kingdom. People who, like all human beings, had some weakness and, perhaps, yielded to some small manifestations of temptation, yet who represented the best of what our Christian culture defined as good and desirable. People like Jean who were young, pretty, wholesome, sweet and who had so much to give to life and to society. People like Jean who had made no major mistakes, unless one could term falling in love and giving all to love a mistake. Yet, people like her were struck down. Certainly, a God of love who demands that mankind surrender to Him and love Him with all his heart would not be so cruel as to strike down an innocent girl for falling in love. Since love is a preserving entity and hate is a destructive entity, how can one reconcile Providence as a power of love when Providence fails to preserve those who work for God and those who are trying to learn to love Him more? Raymond would have concluded that it is a waste of time to love and claim loyalty to a God who destroys without assessing the gravity of the sin.

He could have pointed to people like Buster Jackson, the mill hand who had told Mr. Miles about the fire. Buster boasted that God was all right for church folks who believed in Him, but that he would not give up whiskey and women for all the Kingdoms of Heaven that Christians dreamed of. Buster summed up his view of the Christian hope for a better life in the hereafter: "If God's got anything in Heaven better than whiskey and women, I don't want it." He believed that the blissful feeling that one gets from good corn liquor, and a long lay with a high yellow woman was as near to heaven as a nigger man in Mississippi could ever expect to get. Ever since Raymond was knee high to a duck, he had heard Buster express this philosophy. Buster had lived more than three times as long as Jean—his life was spared while hers was snuffed out. Buster was a maverick, rebelling against all standards of human decency. The lust for illicit flesh was his goal. Yet he lived while the good died. There were many others who fell in Buster's category—persons who committed terrible sins, but who lived. Raymond reasoned that one with control over objects gets rid of the ones he does not want, not the ones he wants. He would have asked, "Does this mean that God lacks the power to select, and that man lives and dies through chance elements and chance elements alone?"

These thoughts of Raymond's remained unexpressed, and perhaps it was better that they did. There are many things that are thought with the greatest inward conviction, but are better not said. While such expression might lighten one's own burden and give peace of mind, they might depress and bring misery and heartache to others.

As Raymond was about to speak, Dr. Sims entered with a radiant smile.

"How are Mr. and Mrs. Miles? I presume you are Raymond's parents."

Without referring to their anxiety about Raymond's condition, Doc Sims said to Raymond, "Do you feel like you could get out of that bed now, young man?"

"Not yet, Doctor, but I feel better now than I did before."

"That's good news," said Doc Sims. "You just keep feeling better and better and we'll have you out of here in little or no time." Making ready for the examination, Doc Sims turned to Mr. and Mrs. Miles and assured them that their boy was in good hands. "Given just a little time, he should be just as good and sound as he was before." In a gentle manner, Doc added, "I know you would stay all night if necessary, but what Raymond needs most of all is rest. We'll have to ask you to leave now. You feel free to come back during visiting hours tomorrow or call us whenever you want to and make inquiries."

"We live too far away to come back tomorrow; however, we'll contact you from time to time. Ida knows how to get in touch with us and can call us, if necessary. So long, Ray, baby," said Mama Miles. "I believe you are in real good hands. When you think about your condition, just thank the Lord, because it could have been worse."

"That's right son," added Papa Miles. "We'll be praying for you, and don't forget to pray for yourself."

As they reached the door, Mama Miles looked back and said, "Don't worry, son, we'll stop by Natchez and take care of everything—just like you said." Her steps quickened as she rushed toward the stairs. Tears were already accumulating in her eyes. "Sweetheart," she said to her husband, "Guess it's nothing we can do but turn our son over to Doc Sims and the Lord."

As the Miles parents left Sweethill hospital, Doctor Sims began his evening examination of Raymond. Raymond's condition was much worse than he had indicated to Mr. and Mrs. Miles. He thought it best not to add to their anxiety.

Chapter V

"Read all about it! Read all about it!" yelled the little white newsboy the next morning. "Two hundred niggers burned to death in a dance hall. Yeh! Read all about it! Two hundred niggers burned to death."

As he walked up and down at the busy intersection looking first one way and then the other, so as not to miss a sale, his rolled-up pant legs revealed yesterday's dirt which heavily covered his bare feet. His uncombed hair falling about his freckled face combined with his language and dress to make passersby classify him as "po' white trash." As he yelled loud and long, there was no doubt about his pronunciation of the word "Negro."

A black couple from Chicago passing through Natchez that day heard the boy's call. As the husband stopped the car, the little boy ran quickly up to it and said, "Paper, Mister?" Hesitating for a moment, the driver said, "Yes" and began searching for a nickel. Disturbed by the boy's headline call, and hoping he would change his pronunciation, the Chicago man asked: "What did you say the headline was?"

"Two hundred niggers burned in dance hall," replied the boy, without a moment's hesitation.

"Look at this damn paper again," retorted the irate driver. "What does it say?" he asked.

"I told you, mister," he said in a frightened voice. "Two hundred niggers burned in dance hall. Don't you see? It's right here. Two hundred people like you."

"Can't you read?" asked the driver.

"Yes, sir."

"Then you see this word," pointing to the word `Negroes'. "It's pronounced `Ne-grows'. Understand?"

"Yes, sir. That's what I said. Two hundred nigras burned in dance hall."

Almost losing control of himself, the driver exclaimed, "You dumb little white cracker bastard. If you were a little bigger, I'd push every one of your teeth down your throat. Let me get the hell out of Mississippi before I get lynched." The little boy quickly backed away from the car as it pulled off amid the honking of horns. Growing up in the segregated culture of Mississippi, the boy did not know that certain words are contemptible when applied to racial groups. On the other hand, the Chicago man did not fully realize that the newsboy was simply a product of his cultural environment—that his expressions were not his own, but the expressions of his group. His references to the so-called Negro race could not go beyond his own socialization. The little boy was not to blame, but rather the society which taught him the vocabulary of racial denigration.

As the car sped toward the outskirts of the city, the driver's wife spoke up. "You know, sweetheart, you did the little boy wrong back there. He didn't mean a bit of harm. He just didn't know any better. He tried hard to say what you wanted him to, but there're too many years of reinforcement. After saying `nigger' for ten or eleven years, to say `Negro' is like speaking a foreign language to him."

"Guess you're right, honey, but he made me as mad as hell. My wanting to punch him in the mouth was my way of showing that I would like to take a potshot at the whole damn white race—at least all those in Mississippi. Not that I would like to hurt anyone in particular, I would just like to knock the props from under the slurs, epithets, and patterns of discrimination upon which the whole ego structure of white superiority is built. While Chicago has its share of racial segregation and discrimination, a man can fight back. You know, in Chicago, a man doesn't have to stand up and let someone call him `nigger' to his face and charge it all off to ignorance. You know yourself, honey, if a southern man, woman or child used the word `Nigger' on the south side, the boys would improve their pronunciation in a matter of minutes. Here in Mississippi, we just take it and say they don't know any better. How long, sweetheart, can intelligent people go on allowing ignorance to triumph? I was always taught that ignorance would vanish in the face of intelligence."

"It will," laughed his wife, "but Mississippi is the exception. So quiet your temper, `old man.' Let me read about two hundred Negroes—mind you, Negroes—who burned to death last night."

"I don't need it read to me. If it's true some white man probably set the fire."

"Hold it, honey. Your prejudice is showing. Wait until you hear the story before you make your judgment. Reporters tend to be honest people whether they are in Mississippi or Illinois."

86

"Okay. You win. I guess I let the little fellow get my goat."

The driver's wife opened the paper and began to read as the car cruised down Highway 61:

> All America was horrified by the disaster at the Rhythm Night Club on St. Catherine Street in which nearly two hundred Negroes lost their lives in the flaming dance hall. A few moments before the first warning wisp of smoke signaled the impending tragedy, these folk were joyous and carefree, eager for fun and frolic, their evening dedicated to happiness. A few minutes later, more than five hundred panic-stricken people were savagely fighting to reach the door. Two hundred of them did not make it.

The newspaper article went on to describe the club as being approximately 200 feet long and 50 feet wide, its top and sides made of corrugated tin. The ceiling was covered with Spanish moss and paper decorations, while all windows except a small one near the front and all doors except the front entrance were barred. Caught in this trap, many burned to death, some died of suffocation, and others were trampled or crushed to death. It was the article's hypothesis that many who were gradually overcome by fumes dropped to the floor unconscious. Meanwhile, flaming bits of moss dropped from overhead to ignite the flimsy dresses of women. As men sought to extinguish the flames rapidly consuming women's dresses, the men's clothes ignited, whereupon they lost all power of reasoning and ran about the hall wildly screaming.

The fire department was summoned immediately from the box across the street. The article complimented the fire unit for acting with great dispatch. According to its description, the firemen arrived on the scene within ten minutes, immediately extinguished the blaze, and rescued many who would otherwise have been lost; many were revived by the use of the pulmotor.

A subsequent news story, however, indicated that perhaps the fire department as well as the police department showed a high degree of irresponsibility. The early paper reported that there had been large-scale looting in the dance hall among the bodies of fire victims. According to the account, men were seen taking watches, wallets and other valuables off the victims. Such theft was characterized as a despicable crime. It was further reported that a molten tin roof fell in on "the hysterical mass of humanity savagely fighting to escape by the one door which opened inward." Thus, hundreds were piled near the door and windows as they scrambled for the main exit or to the outside.

This was the general picture of the Natchez fire received by the Chicago couple who picked up an early edition of the newspaper. After hearing the story, the husband exclaimed, "Don't you see that whites don't give a damn about Negroes! Where was the fire department and police force while all the looting was going on? They don't respect blacks whether they are dead or alive."

"Okay, sweetheart. You're just as prejudiced as they are; only it's in a different form. Suppose we forget this tragedy and try to get to New Orleans safely."

"All right, dear. It makes me so mad to think about it."

For the travelers from Chicago, the Natchez episode was over. They could crowd the memory out of consciousness. For many in Natchez, the tragic fire could not be forgotten. Its impact would follow them forever.

As in the case of many newspaper stories, minor inaccuracies in details occurred. Some papers retracted stories of general looting after both police and those present insisted that whatever looting may have occurred was trivial. The police were complimented in these retractions for throwing the strong arm of protection around this stricken place. It was also found that the tin building was still intact and the roof had not collapsed as had first been reported.

Individual blacks expressed grave concern about the response of the fire department. Some felt that while the advance units arrived quickly, the main fire equipment was much slower to arrive. It was also their feeling that water sprayed inside created a smog, thereby costing more lives. One observer felt that had the fire department concentrated on ripping the hot tin on one side and helping people to safety through the roof, far more lives could have been saved. According to his thinking, "the tin could have easily been ripped from the sides. More air could have entered and more people could have escaped or have been dragged to safety. The whole trouble was nobody wanted to risk his life for Negroes." This observer was not a fireman and perhaps spoke with more sincere belief than authority. Yet, to him and to those who shared his beliefs, it seemed lives had been lost for the lack of speed and efficiency, even though the official evidence indicated that the fire department had acted with efficiency. Speculation on efficiency followed. Investigation after investigation was ordered, examining possible causes and studying the impact of the tragedy.

One thing was certain. The fire was over. The holocaust had left its ugly figure. Irreparable damage had been wrought, especially in the hearts and minds of bereaved families. Efforts were made to assess blame. Newspapermen in search of a story combed every section of the city for informers who had a story to tell. Sundry explanations of how the fire started or of how people escaped were offered freely. While many of these were undoubtedly exaggerated, they were all listened to or read extensively. Whether true or false, any story about the fire attracted attention.

First, the dance hall itself was questioned. Hindsight told everyone that this building, which had served the city for two years as the blacks' largest dance hall, was and had always been a vicious fire trap. Once tragedy struck, it was difficult to find anyone who did not believe that the over-decorated dance hall bore the seeds of its own destruction. Some accepted the thesis that a white man blind with jealousy over the fact that his mulatto mistress was dancing with black men set the fire to "smoke 'em out." Saner groups opined that it had been set accidentally by smokers who violated the "no smoking" rule. The more religious element of the city felt that the fire was the handiwork of the Almighty, expressing his wrath and indignation over the presence of sin. People could not agree on the cause or source of this destruction, but nearly every black family in the city had been touched in varying degrees by this black holocaust.

How did such a barn-like place become a dance hall? First constructed in 1910, it served as a white fraternal hall equipped with adequate exits to accommodate large crowds. Next, it became a stable and a blacksmith shop where the dobbins of wealthy whites were frequently kept, and where the Sunday horses of prosperous farmers came to be shod. Later, the building became a garage for automobiles. For a few years, it housed a firm manufacturing soft drinks. Church workers made much of the idea that Satan visited the place because, after the demise of the beverage industry, it served as a Holiness Church. In 1938, Big Ed Frazier acquired the structure for dance hall purposes and barred up the rear door and all the windows. The only entrance was the front door which led through a hallway to the dance floor. Big Ed lamented the fact that he had to bar the windows and rear door, but experience had shown him that this was the only way to prevent mischievous people from crashing dances. Little did he and the Money Wasters realize that their efforts to save themselves from monetary loss would bring such loss of life to Natchez.

It might easily be argued that the Money Wasters had a right to protect their interests. They had invested their money to create a good place for black entertainment. They had turned an old tin barn-like building into an inviting dance club. The interior had been attractively appointed and arranged; a flawless hardwood floor had been installed; two large exhaust fans provided adequate ventilation; a bar adorned the left side in the back; and beautiful chairs and tables were available for parties. Of course, the club was a firetrap, but it was so much better than anything Natchez blacks had had in the past that they were blind to any dangers. The city fire department had apparently given the building its sanction because it had not been condemned. The fact that the building had the approval of the fire department showed that the department cared little or nothing about the general welfare of blacks, or that it was highly inefficient. Whatever the reason, this fire hazard operated without restrictions.

Exactly how the lethal blaze started will perhaps never be known. Weird stories of narrow escapes were told, some true, others highly exaggerated. Fear frequently distorts perspective, even among those with the best intention of telling the truth.

One man claimed that a girl set the club afire. As two girls emerged from the restroom, he had heard one say to the other, "Girl, you've set the place on fire."

"I don't give a damn," retorted the other girl. "Let's get the hell out of this hole."

The girls then disappeared through the hallway and onto the street—just minutes before the fire was announced. When questioned, the man was unable to give a name or an accurate description of either girl.

On the heels of this story, five black men told of hearing two drunken men mutter something about "going to burn the place down." The men who told this story were promptly apprehended by the police and held for questioning. Since their stories conflicted on whether the drunk set the fire accidentally by flipping a cigarette or by deliberate design and since none of the descriptions coincided very much in details, the police released the men, giving little credence to their stories. The widely circulated story that a jealous white man set the hall afire rarely made its way into the newspapers and no major attempt was made to identify such a person.

One devout Roman Catholic parishioner found his faith in God strengthened after this fiery episode. This man had made plans to attend the dance. While dressing for the dance, he adjusted his crucifix and the clasp broke as he attempted to fasten it. Feeling that he could not go out without his crucifix, he went to the jeweler's shop just as it was closing and pleaded with the jeweler to open up and repair the cross. The jeweler at last opened the shop and repaired the crucifix. The man rushed to the Rhythm Club as fast as he could only to witness a scene of charred desolation. He heard wails of sorrow, smelled the stench of burning flesh, and realized how near he had come to death. Weeping and kissing the crucifix, he cried out: "Oh God! I don't know what I've done to deserve favor. But more than ever I shall dedicate my life to Thee."

The *Louisiana Weekly* of May 5 told a gruesome tale of a nineteen-year-old girl who lived among the dead:

We were standing talking, my friend and I. The band had just stopped playing "Marie" when suddenly we heard screams. We thought it was a fight, but suddenly flame darted through the Spanish moss on the ceiling.

We lost all sense of direction and ran hand in hand toward the bandstand. There was fighting and screaming and some men began cursing and fighting for positions at the barred windows. In the melee, Evelyn and I were torn apart and she tore off a part of my dress. I could hear her calling me and I answered, but we never could get together. The smoke got thick and I began to choke. Something heavy fell against me and I must have been knocked unconscious. When I opened my eyes, I tried to move and could not. My whole body was aching and then I panicked. Everything was dark, but from the odors above me, I could tell that several bodies had fallen on me and I was buried on the floor beneath the dead. I tried to scream but I couldn't.

I could hear somebody above me, gasping and coughing, straining for breath, but at last he gave up the struggle and passed on. A woman whose foot had caught in my dress struggled for a few seconds after I regained consciousness and jerked sharply, muttering, "Lord, have mercy" and shivered to the power of death. I fainted and knew nothing until I was revived outside.

The girl's story indicated that many lost their lives by suffocation. Although many were burned by the leaping flames, the vast majority died from the lack of oxygen. One young lady, a school teacher, was lucky enough to find an adequate air supply in the icebox. Attempting to reach an exit, she found that the crowd had forced her into the refreshment bar. When all apparent hope was gone, she stuck her head into the dance hall's refreshment icebox. She remained conscious until the firemen had gotten the blaze under control and then she fainted. When the last bodies were dragged from the inferno, the school teacher was still breathing, although others in the hall had suffocated. "Why did you put your head in the box? Did you think there was enough oxygen in there to save you?" asked her friends at a much later date.

"No," said the teacher with her unusual sense of humor. "I guess it was my ostrich-like instinct working. I simply hid my head and let the tail wag for itself."

Another teacher at the local high school told a *Pittsburgh Courier* reporter that in the panic people pulled others back from the windows just "like crabs in a barrel." Escaping with a badly burned arm and a deeply gashed leg, she told reporters:

> I am thankful I'm alive. I was near the entrance when some fellow started yelling, cursing and saying that the place was on fire. The crowd had been so dense that dancing was just about impossible and the fire spread over the place almost immediately. My escort climbed up and lifted me to a window, but it was barred shut. Some of the men started to help him break open the window and finally, all working together they pried it open. Then the rush began. Everyone seemed to rush for this one window that was open. Four times I was pushed through the window and was dragged back. Finally, someone grabbed my leg and pulled me through.

One of the most tragic stories of the fire appeared in the May 3 issue of the *Chicago Defender*. The story told of the loss of three of five daughters in one prominent family. Said one of the surviving daughters:

> I was standing near the door talking to Frank Crusten, a friend, when I saw the blaze break out. 'Look, this place is on fire,' I said to him and at that moment he grabbed me by the arm and rushed outside. Once I was outside, I remembered that three of my sisters were inside. I attempted to go back inside, but Frank refused to allow me to go. 'You cannot save them and besides you'll be burned up yourself,' he said to me as I fought desperately to reenter the hall. Then he suggested

that we go home and see if my sisters were there, and the sight of my mother crying and hysterical made matters worse. We returned to the building which was still burning and again I tried to enter but the place was too hot and the smoke too dense to penetrate. Soon the fire ceased and the smoke let up a bit so Father Daugherty, a Catholic priest, took me inside. He and I saw my three sisters burned almost beyond recognition. Their heads were burned bald and, of course, there were no signs of clothing on them—just their charred bodies and enough likeness for identification.

Fortunately, a fourth sister who was temporarily trapped found a way of escape. She remembered that there was a small window in the hall and with almost superhuman force made her way through the crowd toward the window. The window had already been broken out. She plunged headfirst through the window, and four or five others followed in rapid succession. "I was glad all of us did not reach the window at the same time. Maybe we couldn't have agreed which one should go first and we all might have been trapped. As it was, I was burned some but, thanks to my being near the window when the fire broke, not enough to cause me very much pain. The biggest pain I feel is in my heart. If we only had our sisters back . . ."

Out of each crisis, heroes emerge. One of the most noted of those associated with the tragedy of the Rhythm Night Club was James "Boots" Jordan. Boots was employed at the Grand Theater, a large white theater, and was well known to many of Natchez's leading citizens. Eyewitnesses said he was informed of the fire when it first broke out. Being interested in the stage by virtue of his work and fearing the destruction of the property and possibly the life of a fellow showman, he sent orders to the outside for an alarm while he himself attempted to put out the blaze. When it got beyond his control, he made his way to the door, leading several others to safety. Once outside, he secured a weight and reentered with the idea of hammering the bars off some of the windows and permitting others to escape. When the dead were identified, Boots was among them near the base of a window with his improvised hammer still clutched in his hand. Concerning him, the *Natchez Press* commented:

> He got out of the burning building safely, but returned to help others. In doing this, he was trapped by the blaze and burned to death.
>
> True to his training in the theater, he thought of the safety of others before he thought of himself. In an emergency, even though it was not in 'his' theater, he responded in a manner that lived up to the noblest tradition of the profession.
>
> He died that others might live. 'Greater love hath no man than this.'

Perhaps the most outstanding of the heroes were the members of the Walter Barnes band, with Walter the leader of their heroism as well as the leader of their band. The band will long be remembered because it played and tried to restore order long after the fire had been discovered. Just before the fire was discovered, Barnes and his orchestra had played a medley which included "Tuxedo Junction," "Stardust," "Honeysuckle Rose," and was at that moment playing "Marie," a swingy number made famous by Louis Armstrong and revived by the late Jimmie Lunceford.

At first, they thought it was a fight. Learning that it was a fire, Walter said forcefully over the microphone: "Be calm, everybody. Move carefully for the exits." Perhaps Walter Barnes had not taken time to find that there was only one exit—the main door. Directing his band to keep playing, he urged, "Be calm. If you'll all be quiet, everybody will get out safely." Intermittently, he kept playing in an effort to keep the crowd composed. Even when the lights went out, Barnes could be heard saying, "Everybody will get out if we only be calm."

Another person who was reputed to be the last man to leave the inferno alive was Oscar Brown, the drummer in the band. He recalled: "Walter kept us playing. Then the crowd began to rush to the bandstand and I could see that the place was burning rapidly. I yelled to Walter to come on, but he was trying hard to quiet the crowd. When I saw that there was a stampede and the lights were going out, I leaped off the stand and found my way to a window and climbed through. My clothes were torn and my hand was bruised, but I escaped and I thank God for saving my life."

Other members who took the escape route by the nearest window were Jimmie Swift, chauffeur, Chicago; Walter Dillard, valet, Chicago; and Arthur Edwards, bass, Denver. On the other hand, Walter Barnes and nine of his band members died heroically. The *Chicago Defender* said: "Had everyone gotten out of the place, Barnes would have lived as a hero, for those who escaped said he made no move toward the door. The fact that he was found lying near the bandstand is more proof that he thought of others before thinking about himself."

As the news of this tragedy was beamed around the world, news researchers turned back the pages of history for similar disasters. It was soon discovered that the black holocaust in Natchez was the fourth in major fire disasters of the world during the last seventy-five years and the greatest ever suffered by blacks.

The only other disaster in the history of the South that even approaches the tragedy at the Rhythm Night Club occurred in the Shiloh Baptist Church on the night of September 20, 1902. This was the final session of the annual meeting of the National Negro Baptist Convention. Of the crowd of 2,000 to 3,000 men, women, and children who literally packed themselves into this church to worship, 115 were killed and many injured in a stampede when a sudden cry of "fight" was misunderstood for the word "fire."

On this occasion, Booker T. Washington turned out to be something of a prophet. Washington, the founder and then president of Tuskegee Institute, warned that under no conditions should overcrowding be permitted because it was "so dangerous to group safety." The Baptist ministers reasoned that "no man should be turned away from the House of God," thus rejecting the counsel of this prudent educator. Just as Washington finished his address on "Industry," a woman in the choir loft near the rear of the sanctuary who apparently became excited at a momentary jostling near one of the exits suddenly, in a high-pitched voice, shrieked "fight." The word "fire" was passed along rapidly.

Instantly, those who were seated leaped to their feet, rushed for the aisles where for nearly an hour there had been standing room only. In a moment, what had been a sane and orderly group of human beings became a fear-crazed mob with but a single purpose—to get outside. Ignoring, if indeed they ever heard, the words of reassurance of church officials as they shouted from the pulpit that there was no danger, the audience surged toward the front entrance.

Before order could be restored, 115 persons squeezed into the doorway which, though sixteen feet wide, was quickly blocked and with men, women, and children leaping down on them from the balcony, many of those at the doorway were crushed or trampled to death. Even though there was no actual fire in the church, the desire to escape an imaginary inferno was responsible for many deaths.

In the case of the Natchez fire, it was what one person believed that saved his life. Frank Greer, the trumpeter, had a premonition of impending tragedy. He recalled to the *Chicago Defender* that he had predicted disaster several weeks before. Said Greer: "I was riding in a bus and remarked to Barnes that I had a hunch something was going to happen and some of us would be killed." He recalled that "They laughed at me and said I was a crepe hanger."

For compelling reasons, Greer left the band in New Orleans to visit his wife. Probably his intuition caused him to take this action. Whatever the reason, it is likely that he, too, might have been a victim had he been in Natchez.

Many vowed that since God had been so good as to spare their lives, they would never enter another dance hall. One mother openly spoke out against the "cause" which carried so many to an untimely death. She felt that it was the Almighty's way of expressing dissatisfaction with the training mothers were giving their children. She declared: "If more mothers would use the same method I employ, they wouldn't have to worry about such tragedies." She continued, "I keep my daughters at home. I don't like dancing and jitterbugging and no good end will come to those who frequent dance halls and taverns."

Few would have disagreed with her at that time that dance halls were sources of evil. Numerous investigations followed and efforts were made to assure that history would not repeat itself. The mayor promptly placed a ban on all public dancing until the fire department had made the necessary inspections. This act of "locking the stable after the horse had gone" benefitted the whites, in the main, for there were no other large dance halls for blacks in the city. How many persons were in the hall perhaps will never be known definitely, for only one man, Ed Frazier, owner of the club and vice president of the Money Wasters' Club, knew this fact. He collected and tabulated tickets and he alone knew the exact number. He was a victim of the fire. Rumors had it that "Big Ed" had gotten out and discovered that in his excitement he had left his money. He returned to the flaming building to collect his money, only to be consumed by the fire. While the loss of Big Ed in death was unfortunate, one observer felt that it was fortunate for Ed, as well as for the city, that he died that way. This observer said: "Big Ed Frazier's death saved the city another tragedy. If the fire hadn't killed him, the niggers would have. Many people who lost children and husbands and wives and other relatives came looking for him with blood in their eyes. If they had found him, they would have lynched him on the spot. His number was up that night. The only thing I'm glad of is that the fire beat them to him. It'd been too bad to have niggers lynch another nigger in Mississippi."

Whether this appraisal of behavior was correct or not can perhaps never be proved, yet it is true that in this crisis, a scapegoat was sought.

The fire department, which the city said acted with efficiency and dispatch, bore its part of the criticism. However, when accused of lethargy and neglect by a not-too-silent public, it is not always enough to receive a clean bill by officials. Thus, the Natchez mayor put in a second request for a salaried fire marshall to be employed by the Natchez City Council. Seeking to relieve himself and the fire department of some of the blame, he said, "If I had been supplied with a fire marshal as I asked when I took office, the terrible fire on the 23rd might have been avoided."

100

No fire marshal had been hired, the dance hall firetrap had not been inspected, and 209 blacks had died. Placing the blame might satisfy some desires of the living, but it would not bring back the dead. The dead had been consumed in the black holocaust—offered as sacrificial souls to the evil gods of racial segregation.

Chapter VI

Thursday morning, April 25th, less than thirty-six hours after the tragic fire, the quiet city of Natchez began the heartbreaking task of burying its dead. The first funeral—of an unidentified man—was held at ten o'clock. Within a half hour, six additional funerals were held and before twilight Natchez was the scene of more black funerals per hour than its average six-month total.

Fortunately, the three black mortuaries in the city were all located within two blocks of the Rhythm Night Club, making transportation of the victims an easier task. So small and unprepared were these funeral parlors for such a catastrophe that bodies had to be stacked in every available space. At first, it was supposed that the three establishments would be unable to fulfill their obligations since more than forty percent of all black families in Natchez held membership in burial associations. These associations, which formed the core of each funeral parlor, were obligated to bury all members without cost. Under this arrangement, normal deaths could be handled easily and expeditiously by each firm, but periods of disaster were likely to create responsibilities beyond their means. The Red Cross, however, announced that it would assume financial responsibility up to seventy-five dollars for burial of all fire victims whose survivors were unable to pay. A fund of $25,000 was set up for this purpose.

In this time of tragedy, the city of Natchez tried to find within the limits of its social structure a modicum of humaneness. For a short while, color barriers were broken and blacks and whites worked together in aiding grief-stricken families. In the midst of crisis, people seemed to have forgotten that there were such differences as color of skin and texture of hair. There was only one great difference manifested—most white families were alive and intact, while black families, almost without exception, were touched with grief.

Wealthy white women worked side by side with poorer black women and men who gave their assistance to the inadequate public health staff in administering lockjaw treatments, filling out reports, assigning orphans, or supervising funeral arrangements. They cried, empathized, and tried to console many of their darker brothers and sisters. One white woman, looking down on Jean Gravier's lifeless body, could no longer hold back her tears. "Oh, what a lovely child," she cried. "She could have easily been my daughter—and she had to die in a place like this!"

How right she was. Jean had all the Caucasian features of the white woman. She was fair, pretty and cultured. Economically, she would have been assigned to the middle class in any society. Physically, she could have passed for white. Yet, because of caste—because of her identification with the black race—she was forced to attend the best black social club in the city—the Rhythm Night Club. In her grief and feelings of guilt, this wealthy white woman was searching for the rationale which underlay biracial patterns in Mississippi. Here was a girl who was just as "white" as she, dead because society had forced her to search for enjoyment in a firetrap. Here was a girl who could trace her heritage back to a slave grandmother who was a victim of the white man's exploitation—loved by night and hated by day. As she looked on Jean's lifeless body, she did not really know whether she cried at the death of a stranger or at the death of a kinswoman. Part of her emotional reaction was born of guilt—not for herself alone, but for the whole white race.

Other whites undoubtedly had a similar feeling, for in practically every area of life the color line was crossed. Blacks not immediately grieved by losses in the fire could almost wish for some continuing crisis in Natchez that would maintain racial peace and cooperation. Many whites undoubtedly realized for the first time that blacks were human beings who laughed, cried, bled and died just as they did. Many whites saw for the first time the deplorable social conditions in which black people lived and had compassion for them. Perhaps they realized that indirectly they had laid the groundwork for this black holocaust. In an effort to make amends, to soothe guilty consciences, white newspapers offered their full facilities to black newspapermen and white editors wrote editorials commending acts of heroism and appealing for financial and moral support. White undertakers made cars and portions of their facilities available to black morticians and businessmen gave both their time and money to the cause. The most despotic of all elements in the city, the police, did all that was possible to maintain order and at the same time show respect for the dead.

Public-spirited citizens, predominantly white, rallied to the cause. The mayor and his business associates gave the first fifty dollars toward a relief fund. It was not long before the fund reached $5,000. In addition to his personal gift, the mayor lent his weight of office to a campaign to raise additional funds.

The mayor's proclamation issued Wednesday afternoon after the fire read:

> Whereas, our community has suffered a major disaster in the terrible occurrence wherein several hundred of our colored citizens have died and have suffered serious injury—and—
>
> Whereas, it is imperative that a large sum of money be collected at once with which to assist the injured and in the immediate burial of those killed—and—
>
> Whereas, on account of the disaster that has befallen the community, a situation of extreme emergency now exists—
>
> Now, therefore, I, W.J. Byrne, Mayor of the City of Natchez, do hereby call upon all citizens of Natchez and Adams County and this community to voluntarily contribute funds to the very best of their ability and I do hereby designate the Adams County Chapter of the American Red Cross as the agency to collect and disburse funds collected.

Realizing the suffering and heartache of many of her neglected citizens, the Mississippi House of Representatives voted 99 to 27 to donate $2,000 of state funds to the Adams County Chapter of the American Red Cross to alleviate suffering resulting from the fire disaster. The funds were to be used toward hospitalization of the injured and the burial of the dead.

No one could deny that many whites showed an increased degree of understanding and compassion. Nevertheless, this display of brotherly love was too little and too late for many. As one leading black citizen appraised the situation:

> It's a case of locking the barn door after the horse is gone. Or better still, of bringing the doctor after the patient is dead. Suppose the City of Natchez had given $5,000 and the House of Representatives had given $2,000 for the purpose of building a safe place for the recreation of Negroes. Suppose Negroes could

have been provided with a decent place like the whites have for themselves. This fire would never have been. Yet, after many of my people burn to death in that hellhole, they come around crying and saying they are sorry. They put up a few dollars and expect colored people to be duped into thinking they love them. To me, it was not the person who accidentally set the place afire who is to blame. It's the whole pattern of segregation. By clinging to their superior attitudes and forcing us into dumps and dives, they are just as guilty of starting that fire as if they had struck the match. I hate to say it, but it is an indirect case of mass homicide.

Regardless of the conditions which caused the fire, regardless of the existence of the biracial system, for a while at least, most of Natchez's black citizens had to be preoccupied not with the living but the dead. With the assurance of funds from the Red Cross and contributions by individuals and the state, morticians worked feverishly embalming all bodies brought to their firms. From Thursday through Tuesday of the next week an average of forty funerals per day were held. The almost continuous funeral processions, escorted by white motorcycle police, made their way to the woefully small, segregated cemetery.

Individual graves were the rule as far as possible. The WPA joined voluntary workers in digging graves. There were some common graves. Members of the same family or close kindred were buried in common graves. In some cases where individual families were unable or unwilling to assume any financial responsibility, their dead shared common graves—often with strangers or unidentified victims. Some people said those who shared a common grave shared a common eternity. This baffled many laymen as well as the ministers who preached the funerals. It was the ministers who had to take a public stand.

The funerals were difficult to preach. As a matter of fact, some ministers refused to officiate at the funerals of people who in their view had already been condemned to hell. Most ministers in the Natchez vicinity were by training and orientation strict fundamentalists, and they found it extremely perplexing to preach such funerals. Should they follow their religious convictions and condemn the dead to eternal damnation or should they preach a sermon which would give the bereaved some hope of seeing their loved ones "on that great-getting-up morning"?

Some ministers took the latter approach while others followed traditional beliefs. The Reverend Matthew Jaggert believed sincerely in the reality of a burning hell and that the wicked were certain to be "punished with everlasting separation from the presence of the Lord"; however, he judged it unwise to emphasize this point. The Reverend Jaggert was a young, skinny, slightly bald, brown-skinned man of about thirty years of age. He had been trained in one of the best black colleges, Leland College, and represented the progressive wing of the ministry in the city. He had pastored his church for about two and one-half years and was gaining little by little the cooperation of the "old pillar" element of the church. One of the big criticisms against him was that he was too educated— that he had had to go to college just to learn how to preach. If those first years in the pulpit had taught Jaggert anything, they had taught him that "college preaching" had no place in his church. Even though his church could boast of one of the highest educational levels in the city, they had not outgrown a certain dependence upon highly emotional religious services. Matthew Jaggert knew that this day demanded neither emotionalism nor fundamentalism, but rather tact and understanding. It demanded that Christianity be made practical—that the minister realize that traditional beliefs are sometimes destructive to harmony and solidarity.

In this situation, the young minister sought the advice of one of the older deacons. He inquired, "Brother Jones, what would you preach if you were me?"

Brother Jones replied, "All I have to say, Reverend, is I'm just glad I ain't in your shoes. Just preach what the Spirit tells you to."

"Thank you, Brother Jones," said Jaggert as he walked a few steps away, deep in thought. Suddenly, he turned and said to Deacon Jones, "You know, Deacon, it is impractical to preach a sermon of damnation for the funeral services of sons and daughters of fathers and mothers who are the mainstays of the church both financially and spiritually." He paused for a minute and continued, "Such a thing would spell spiritual ruin for the congregation, economic suicide for the general church program, and financial ruin for the minister. It takes a stronger religious conviction than I have, Brother Jones, to kill that many valuable things at one time. Maybe the Lord will tell me what course to take before two o'clock."

"I know He will," said Brother Jones. "You know, He said He'd make a way out of no way."

As Jaggert sat in his study, a text came to him which would allow him to assume a middle-of-the-road position—"Judge not that ye be not judged."

That afternoon, when Matthew Jaggert arose to deliver his sermon, his anguish was apparent in his face. He knew deep down that he was compromising his convictions, and hence the word of God, to please men. Nevertheless, he continued. With words calculated to offend no one, he began his sermon:

Man is finite. His judgment is superficial and inadequate. God alone, who has an all-seeing eye and can view the past, present, and the future at a glance, can say where man will spend eternity. Today, we have come to pay our last respects to young members of our church and some old ones, too, who were snatched from our midst by the omnipotent hand of the Almighty. The circumstances by which they left us, I need not repeat. We all know them too well. Where will they spend eternity? It is not for us to say. Jesus says, 'Judge not that ye be not judged.'

All of you remember my father who pastored this fine congregation before me. Many of you have heard him use this illustration. You remember he used to tell about the sinful man who was riding his horse home from the beer joint one evening and his horse jumped to avoid stepping into a hole. The man was thrown headfirst from the horse and was killed immediately. But, before he hit the ground, he said, 'Lord, have mercy.' My father declared that that man is in heaven, for with God, there is room between the stirrup and the ground. If God saved this sinner, I know he will save his children who have known and loved Him.

The dead over which we mourn were reared in Christian homes and nurtured in the Christian church. No one will deny that they died under questionable circumstances—that at that particular time, they were backsliders. Yet, only a doubting Thomas would question the power of God to save. All things are possible with God. Those of you who would render final judgment, a task of which you are incapable, I invite you to take a look at the dying thief on the cross. Although he had never been baptized, a symbol of Christianity which we consider necessary, in a critical moment the thief called on the Lord. Said he, 'Master, when thou come into Thy kingdom, remember me.' Jesus Christ, the Son of the living God, said, 'today, you shall be with me in Paradise.'

Here was a man who had been a social outcast; a parasite on society; a flouter of all social conventions; a deviate by all societal standards; an obvious candidate for hell—yet, in the nick of time, he decided finally to call on God. God answered the call and my Bible tells me that he was invited to join Christ in Paradise.

But we all know that those who have gone to rest were members in regular church attendance here nearly every Sunday. Although they had been tempted by the devil and momentarily yielded to temptation, how many of us could say that people who had once known God and His love could completely forget Him? I do believe that in their moments of agony—in their Gardens of Gethsemane—they prayed for God to remove their bitter cups. They asked the Lord to 'Have mercy on me.' And I, for one, find a great deal of consolation in my belief that he who calls on the Almighty can be 'saved between the stirrup and the ground.' Certainly, God would not be so merciful as to save a dying thief who had never given him any love or honor and turn a deaf ear to hundreds of his children who were guilty only of momentary hypocrisy.

We have seen God call from among us many of those who were dear to us by methods which we did not approve. But we all know that God moves in a mysterious way. Maybe he took the few as a test of faith of the many of us who survive. Maybe he took them as a warning to us to turn away from our many sins. Maybe, since most were young people, it was not their sins but the sins of the forefathers being wrought upon successive generations. Maybe we did not set the right examples. Maybe we left the path cluttered with temptation to which the young or immature mind would be prone to yield. Kahlil Gibran, a religious man but not a Christian, writing in his famous book, *The Prophet,* uttered these words which all of us should ponder in our hearts:

> And when one of you falls down, he falls for those
> behind him, a caution against the stumbling stone. Ay,
> and he falls for those ahead of him who, though faster
> and surer of foot, yet removed not the stumbling stone.

Listen to me, my sisters and brethren, before we indict, before we condemn, let us examine our own hearts. Have we always lived in such manner that we would be ready to meet our God at whatever time he called? Looking back over our own lives, how many of us, with clear conscience, could cast the first

110

stone? Christians will agree that this is not a time for incrimination and condemnation, but a time for prayer—prayer for heavenly consolation for the bereaved families and prayer that God will receive our own, His own, into His kingdom. . . .'Judge not that ye be not judged. Judgement is mine said the Lord.'

The Reverend Matthew Jaggert felt he had preached a sermon God would have had him preach. A good sermon, whether inspired by life or death, is supposed to motivate hope. Hope for a better life in this world; hope for the resurrection of the dead; hope that in the hereafter, we will meet our loved ones and will know each other. Using a mature intellectual and religious approach, had he not produced a sermon of consolation as well as challenge? Had he not followed the mandates of Christianity—love, compassion, forgiveness, hope for resurrection and complete dependence upon an omnipotent God? Although he was satisfied, he was realistic enough to know that even though his members nodded their heads in approval as he spoke, they did not fully understand nor appreciate his religious outlook.

As they filed out from the funeral service, most stopped to compliment Reverend Jaggert. People were heard to say: "He preached the best sermon he could under the circumstances," or "He sure had a difficult sermon to preach," or "I would not have wanted to be in Reverend Jaggert's shoes." These comments gave open approval while nods gave tacit approval. Yet, in a Bible belt region where literalism and obscurantism provided the heart of the fundamentalist's approach, surely many who heard this sermon left feeling still that "the wicked shall be punished with everlasting separation from the presence of God."

A self-made, "God-called" minister, the Reverend Adam Mellon, officiated at a mass funeral for fire victims. His message, in contrast to that of Matthew Jaggert, was one of absolute fatalism. He stood looking grimly out at his congregation. There was a tenseness in the congregation, for the Reverend Mellon was known to be a preacher who would "speak the truth." He was a large, fat, ebony man about fifty years old who conformed to most of the regional stereotypes of the uneducated black minister, with his slightly hoarse voice, his graying hair, and a large gold chain and watch fob adorning his black serge suit. People would whisper jokingly when he passed: "If it wasn't for that white collar around his neck, you couldn't tell where the suit started or stopped."

Remarks about his color, his dogmatic Christian beliefs, or his actions in the community did not seem to disturb the Reverend Mellon at all. He made no apologies for being black. "Doesn't black stand out?" he would ask. "Isn't a black diamond the most valuable? Isn't a blackberry the sweetest? Wasn't it a black man that bore Christ's cross up Calvary? Wasn't Jesus himself black? The Bible said that 'His hair shall be like wool' and only black men have wooly hair. So you know I'm glad to be black because that makes me more like the Master."

His congregation would respond with "Amen, Amen."

Although Mellon had never been to college or even high school, everybody gave him credit for knowing his Bible. He believed everything that one did had to be justified by the Bible. He often boasted that no "college-sent" minister could "hold a candle to him" because he was a "God-sent" preacher. He could quote almost any passage in the Holy Book and often challenged other ministers to prove him wrong. He openly stated that his denomination was the only church and all others were lost. In addition to knowing the Word, Mellon tried to live within the letter of the Bible. He did not smoke, drink, nor chase after the sisters. He could call on any member in his congregation to stand up and tell the others if they had ever seen him sin. In twenty years, no one could remember anyone calling his hand. His congregation hoped that for this one time he would be considerate of the bereaved.

Mellon pulled out his gold pocket watch, snapped open the lid, and put it back in his pocket. Those who knew him well knew that this did not mean a thing because he was going to take as much time as he wanted to anyway. Staring seriously over the congregation, he began:

> Sisters and brethren, we won't be here long today. I have been called upon to preach the funeral of the deceased. But a preacher of the Gospel is supposed to bring good news—good news even in death. But today, there is no good news—there is no ray of hope, for those who departed the way of life have obviously been condemned to hell. The Bible tells us so. In search for a text suitable for this occasion, I've called upon the Book of Revelation. 'Even as Sodom and Gomorrah, and the cities about them in like manner, giving themselves over to fornication, and going after strange flesh, are set forth for an example, suffering the vengeance of eternal fire.' Subject: "You Must Give An Account in Judgement. Say Amen, brothers.

A feeble reply came from the congregation.

> Just a couple of nights ago, God stepped out of the blue up yonder and snatched from among us our own sons and daughters who were seeking 'strange flesh' in a dance hall owned and operated by the devil. Most of these sinful souls had their names on the church roster, but we know now that their names were not written up there. Thus, they can expect no good life in the hereafter, but like any other sinner, they'll have to give an account in judgment. They are in a bad predicament. The fact that they had once known God in the pardoning of their sins and went back on His Word makes them worse than an infidel.

It is high time for those of us who profess to be Christians to realize that we cannot play with God. The Word is so clear that even a fool can't err. God has told us that and every Christian knows it. If you serve God for twenty-three hours of the day and mess up and sin the last hour, you aren't going to heaven and you needn't expect to because hell is going to be your portion. Amen. Say Amen, Church.

.Again the church said "Amen," but very softly—and some members even covered their mouths so that bereaved friends and relatives would not see or hear them. Few wanted to say openly that their friends' sons or daughters were hopelessly condemned. Consequently, a group that was known for its "talking back to the preacher" was unusually quiet. Today, they responded only to direct calls for "Amens." Adam Mellon continued in his gravelly voice:

God's children must always walk the straight and narrow path. There are no hooks and crooks that one might take on this pilgrim journey. He has purposely set the devil loose in the world to tempt man from every side. Amen. But he tells his children just as plain as the nose on your face 'yield not to temptation.' He who yields is guilty of sin. Yet, we all know 'the wages of sin is death, but the gift of God is eternal life through Jesus Christ our Lord.' Amen. You know, sisters and brothers, you can take off the clothes of mortality and put on the clothes of immortality only if you die free from sin. Immortality is God's gift to all men who find and keep Jesus. If you lose him and die in sin, it is no two ways about it, you're going to wake up in hell. Amen.

The fact that these dead died in a flaming dance hall—a place which from the beginning was a chosen agent of hell—showed that they had pushed Jesus aside. And brothers and sisters, Hallelujah! When a man or woman pushes Jesus aside, he's a lost ball in high cotton and in high gear on the downward road. Amen. Regardless of who they were—mine or yours—the truth must be preached. They had backslid at the time of their death. They had fallen from the boundless grace of God.

Amen. They were sinners living slap dab in the middle of sin. Sin denies immortality and once that is denied, brother, you must suffer eternal damnation in an everlasting fire. Amen.

About that time, Mellon had begun to hum, holler or, as his congregation would say, he had begun to preach:

Hum-m-m, brothers and sisters, Amen. Don't you take lightly the fact about souls burning in eternal fire. Let's see what the Bible says about it. The Bible compares the wicked to chaff, stubble, and wax which will one day be consumed in a burning fire. I can hear John 3:36 say, 'Christ will gather his wheat in the garner, but he will burn the chaff with unquenchable fire.' Listen with me, brothers and sisters, as we hear Matthew 3:12 say: 'For behold, the day cometh, that shall burn as an oven and all you proud, yes, all that do wicked shall be stubble.' Again, Malachi 4:1 plainly says, 'As smoke is driven away, so drive them away; as wax melteth before the fire, so let the wicked perish at the presence of God.' Amen. Let me hear somebody say Amen.

Again faint "Amens" came forth. Disturbed at this half-hearted response, the Reverend Mellon continued:

Some of you act like you blame me for preaching the Gospel. You have heard the Bible speaking about eternal damnation in an unquenchable fire. Your preacher didn't say that; the Bible said so. Amen. Hallelujah! Don't say I preached anyone to hell. God has prescribed the medicine; it is bitter, but it's what the ailment calls for. Regardless of what we may think, none of us can change one iota of what God has prescribed. For those of us left, we should be thankful. God has shown us His wrath. This has come as a warning to all of us. Thus, we must always live so we will be ready. Nothing we can do will save our deceased from the punishment they deserve. This sermon is for you, the living. It is God's way of telling you through me to be ever ready—for no one knows when He calls. Remember, brothers and sisters, just let us be ready when he calls.

Then, with his usual form of closing a sermon, he burst abruptly into song:

If the master calls me, I will answer,/ I will answer, I will answer./ If the master calls me, I will
answer,/ I'll be somewhere working for the Lord.

The congregation, which had been unusually quiet for a
funeral, suddenly began to give forth emotional outbursts.
Relatives yelled and some became hysterical or fainted. Yet,
the greater the emotional reaction, the louder the Reverend
Mellon sang. In addition to losing relatives, there was the
added grief of knowing that loved ones had been doomed to
eternal damnation. This was more than most of the bereaved
could bear.

The sermon was over. As had been expected, Reverend
Mellon had "spoken the truth." Most who came to pay their
last respects agreed that the Reverend Mellon had been too
hard on the bereaved families. One member was heard to say,
"If he had been preaching over one of my kids, I would have
gotten up and walked right up in the pulpit and stuck my fist
in his big mouth. He stands there and tries to make the people
think he is perfect—think he God Almighty. If there is no pressing reason why one should tell the truth, then he should spare
others heartache. He might know the Bible, but he's a fool
where human nature is involved, if you ask me."

As the members filed out of the church, few stopped to
congratulate Adam Mellon. One of the old pillars of the church
was heard to say, "You know, it just wasn't any need for Reverend Mellon saying all the things that he did. Of course, they
were all the truth, but sometimes there ain't no good in telling
the truth. Even Jesus spared the woman who was guilty of
adultery some embarrassment. You know, it might be good
that God ain't a black man. He would have no mercy on anyone. The least little thing they do, they would be sent to hell."

"I agree with you," replied another longtime member. "There wasn't any need for all of that—even though it's true. I would have hated some kind of bad to have been a member of one of the families. I might have lost my religion right there in church and choked the—if you excuse me—choked the hell out of him."

Both laughed softly and disappeared in the crowd.

It seemed that most people felt that the Reverend Mellon had told the truth. No one could deny it because, as he so clearly pointed out, it was right there in the Bible. Nevertheless, most would have agreed with the two old pillars of the church. In Christian life, an act of omission is sometimes called for. There are times, places, and circumstances in which the truth should not be told. In fact, a lie is just as good as the truth if it is used in the right place. Perhaps Mellon could have told a lie and rushed out of the pulpit and asked the Lord to forgive him. Had he done that, he could have brought a ray of hope to the depressed souls who bore the burden of their tragic losses. If a sermon destroys hope, if it destroys faith in the Almighty to overcome the evils of any worldly situation, then it is worse than a message from an infidel.

Almost a week of heartaches and suffering passed. One observer stated that blacks in the City of Natchez had shed enough tears to float a battleship. Self-righteous ministers like the Reverend Mellon and others did little to soothe the wounded spirits. As fundamentalists they interpreted Bible passages literally and acted accordingly. Few in Natchez will ever forget the action of one semi-literate minister at the cemetery. As he was returning the bodies to the dust of the earth from which they came, he felt that a minister should not dignify the burial of sinners by looking down on them. Thus, he turned his back ceremoniously on the grave, explaining that Jesus had advised Satan to "get ye behind me." Since this was the work of Satan, he (Satan) was present in the grave. He turned his back to put Satan in his place.

Once the news of this act spread, many of the citizens were irate. One citizen said if he had been present at the cemetery, he would have pushed that self-righteous son-of-a-bitch in the grave and thrown dirt in on him. This perhaps summed up what the majority of the people felt. These were unusual times. They had faced a crisis of undreamed magnitude. They had acted as people do in time of crisis—intelligently, unintelligently, rationally, irrationally, bravely, fearfully.

By Friday of the next week, practically all funerals were over. In the main, they had been carried out efficiently with dignity and solemnity. Regardless of the action of ministers and the dictates of fundamentalist doctrines, the *Natchez Press* carried the following comment on its front page for the issue of May 2:

> In spite of the unprecedented number of burials, the funerals were conducted with dignity and solemnity that was a marked tribute to the Negro race and brought fortitude to the bereaved families of the deceased.

Conspicuous among those who were buried was Jean Gravier. Raymond's condition would not permit him to attend, but Papa and Mama Miles and his sister assured him that they would be there. Her funeral was quiet and solemn. Papa Miles was a little disturbed because it was a Roman Catholic funeral and no one was given a chance to say anything over the body. It seemed so heartless not to permit some few people to point up the good that a person had done while living. He did not know what he was going to say, but he had planned to say something on behalf of his son and the Miles family had he been given a chance. He had gotten a beautiful spread of flowers made in the shape of Raymond's initials

After the funeral, Papa and Mama Miles made their way to the Gravier home. Mama Miles spoke:

"I know this is a bad time to come to call on you, but I couldn't leave town without telling you that I feel like I have lost a daughter," said Mrs. Miles. "Raymond wanted us to be here. You know you have our sympathy and prayers."

"Thank you," said Mrs. Gravier. "I'm glad you came."

"You know," said Mrs. Miles, "Raymond doesn't want to get well. He's eating his heart out and blaming himself for Jean's death. Although he is living, he will never be the same."

"You tell him for me, and please make him believe it, that neither I nor Mr. Gravier blame him for what has happened and he must not blame himself. In fact, tell him that we'll be up to see him next week. This is God's world and He knows what's best."

"Thank you. I can't help but cry when I say this, but you would have made a wonderful mother-in-law for my son."

"We loved your boy," said Mrs. Gravier. "He was every inch a man with good home training. I pray to God he gets better. He's always welcome in our home."

"We are so glad to hear you say that. We must be going now. I feel that we have already disturbed you too long. Good-bye and God bless you."

"Good-bye and do come again whenever you are in Natchez," said Mrs. Gravier.

As Papa and Mama Miles made their way toward the car, tears were in their eyes. Mother Miles spoke up, "Aren't they wonderful people? They have such big hearts."

"Yes, they are among the best people I ever met. But you know, I don't see how my emotions will let me describe this funeral to Raymond. Jean didn't look like she was dead. She was just as pretty as she ever was. She just looked like she was asleep. What a thin line it must be between the sleep of life and the sleep of death."

"Let's not start worrying again. It's all over now and there's nothing we can do. Let's start back toward Corapeake before it gets too dark. It'll probably be a good while before people in this town will be the same again."

Unfortunately, cooperation and crisis left Natchez at the same time. As the hearses ceased their unpleasant rumbling across the city, black-white relations resumed their usual tenor. Many of those who had cooperated so beautifully returned to their traditional caste patterns. Natchez gradually returned to normal, to the segregation and discrimination which had laid the groundwork for the black holocaust at the Rhythm Club.

Chapter VII

As Raymond lay in the hospital, he had ample time to reflect on the short but wonderful time he and Jean had shared. He also had ample time to blame himself for her death. At first, he tried desperately to accept her death as an inevitable part of a divine plan, hoping to rid himself of guilt and find solace through reminiscence. Whenever he was left alone, he tried not to see a Jean caught up by the horrors of death, but a beautiful, vivacious Jean who had for two years brightened his life. Unconsciously, he was striving to make her a "phantom lover" in order to escape reality.

Thinking of their two years together, Raymond recalled how he and Jean had met. In the freshman orientation program at Sweethill College, the young men would walk one way and the young ladies another. After skipping for about two revolutions, at the sound of a whistle each young man was supposed to introduce himself to the young lady in front of him and hold her in conversation for one minute. This process was repeated until there was a reasonable possibility that most had had an opportunity to meet.

In this rotation, Raymond met many young ladies. But he knew that life had started anew for him when he stopped in front of young Jean Gravier. Although he had vowed to his high school sweetheart back home that he would not even look at another girl in college, he knew at that moment that his vow must be broken. Gazing into Jean's eyes, Raymond found himself speechless. After a few seconds, he muttered, "My name's Raymond Miles. What's yours?"

A soft, penetrating voice replied, "Jean Gravier, and I'm from Natchez. Where are you from?"

Feeling somewhat ashamed of his small country village, Raymond's first thought was to name a larger city. Before he could, however, he realized that he must be honest with Jean. He answered truthfully, "Corapeake. Bet you don't know where that one-horse town is."

"Oh yes," said Jean. "We have some distant relatives living out in your country about forty miles southeast of Natchez. I passed through your hometown once and it didn't look like a one-horse town to me."

"That's kind of you," said Raymond, "but you must admit that it's small." At that point, the conversation stopped. For the next few seconds, they just stood there looking into each other's eyes. Perhaps those few seconds of intense searching into the feelings and warmth that beamed from the eyes of each brought them closer together than words could ever have done. Just as the line was beginning to move again, Raymond spoke up: "You know, you're a very pretty girl and I like you very much." Time would not permit her to answer, but her parting smile assured Raymond that the feeling was mutual.

During orientation week, Raymond did not get an opportunity to talk with Jean. The policy of separation of young men from young women was strictly enforced. Freshman girls, dressed in their blue denim uniforms, were not permitted to socialize on campus except on Saturday afternoons and Sundays. Nevertheless, whenever Raymond and Jean met, they exchanged unusually warm smiles. From Tuesday until Saturday, this was the extent of their relationship.

On Saturday, as Raymond was leaving lunch, he bumped into Jean. Strangely enough, Raymond had wanted to avoid Jean that day because the Freshman Hop was being held that night and he knew he couldn't dance. When he met Jean, perhaps his expression was not as warm as it might have been because he feared she would ask him about the dance.

"Hi, Ray. Where's that big smile today?"

"Hi, Jean. Since I'm not feeling very well, I guess I left it inside."

"You're still feeling good enough to have a sense of humor," said Jean. "Perhaps if you walk out on the campus awhile, you'll feel better. This is Saturday afternoon, you know."

Strolling across the campus, their green freshman caps bright in the brilliant sun, they shared their experiences of freshman week. Jean recalled the humiliation of wearing long plaits with a bow tied on the end of each and wearing her ugly blue uniform inside out. Raymond mourned the loss of his long pompadour which he had spent years growing—the upperclassmen had shaved his head as clean as a billiard ball.

In due course, the question of the dance arose. Jean asked, "Who are you taking to the dance tonight?"

Ray paused a minute. "Since I have a headache, I had just about decided not to go."

"Don't say that, Ray," said Jean. "go home and lie down and you'll find later that dancing will be good relaxation for you."

Raymond kicked a little clump of grass underneath the huge, moss-covered oak. "Well . . . dancing would not be relaxation for me. You see, I can't dance. I hated to tell you because I sort of hoped you would have wanted me to take you to the dance. Would you have wanted me to take you to the dance? You see, I knew it wouldn't be any fun with me. That's why I was running away and hiding behind a headache."

Jean laughed briskly. "Ray, you are a card. You don't know much about ladies, do you? I would enjoy being with you if you never danced a step. Since your religion doesn't keep you from dancing, then I'll enjoy teaching you how. So to settle it all, I'll say, `We have a date at eight for the dance.' Okay?"

"Yes," said Raymond, feeling greatly relieved. "I warn you that I'm a country clodhopper so you had better watch out for your toes."

"Don't worry about me," she laughed. "Jean knows the art of looking out for herself—especially where country boys are concerned. So just go on to your room and rest, and I'll see you at eight."

The evening was beautiful. Jean taught Raymond to dance. First, she taught him how to "slow drag" and before the evening was over, he was trying to "swing out." Raymond was a quick learner and Jean an eager teacher. Jean remarked that Raymond learned the steps amazingly fast despite following the six-inches-apart rule. Raymond thought that the ease with which they danced showed that they were meant for each other.

Over the year, the two became inseparable. They both majored in business, and had all classes together except physical education. He met her at seven for breakfast and escorted her to her dormitory at sunset each evening. The boys teased him for not allowing Jean time "to go to the restroom."

Raymond reflected on how long that first summer had seemed and how much he had wanted to travel from Corapeake to Natchez to see Jean. Although it was only forty-odd miles away, he did not have the money or the transportation to go see her. Only her frequent letters brightened his rural existence. When the new school term began, he remembered how proud he was, for once more he would be with his beloved Jean.

During their sophomore year their attachment deepened. His new scholarship plus his summer earnings gave him a few extra pennies. In addition to that, Raymond made friends with Jimmie, a boy from Natchez who had an old car and was good at shooting "the ole bones." Whenever he was broke, Raymond would "stake" him and he would thus share his winnings with Raymond. Jimmie was a "slickster" and the greenhorns from small hick towns would likely be taken in by him. So, to Raymond, staking him was as good as money in the bank: with this new source of income, Raymond could visit Jean who occasionally went home on weekends.

There had been many good weekends with Jean in Natchez. Raymond would stay at Jimmie's house nearby and they would make the weekends as full as possible. Mama and Papa Gravier were learning to like Raymond. He recalled the day he was first introduced to the family. Father, mother, grandmother, and children were on hand, all fair-skinned. The grandmother said, "Stand up, son," then proceeded to walk around him. She observed his well-developed body, his Indian complexion, and his black curly hair. As Raymond stood there, he felt a close kinship with slaves on the auction block long ago. After looking him over, grandma spoke again. "He seems like a nice, well-mannered boy. He's a little . . ."—she could not find the last word—"But he has good hair."

Raymond surmised that the word she was looking for was "black," but he was too much in love with Jean to let that make any difference. After the family put its stamp of approval on Raymond, he and Jean were left alone. Raymond said to Jean, laughingly, "My hair is all right, but I'm just too black."

Jean retorted: "She did not say that, Raymond Miles. They all like you. I've been living with them for seventeen years, and I know their likes and dislikes. You're in, young man, you are in with the family. You'll have to find another excuse if you want to find another girl. Besides, you're not black, you're tantalizing tan, and that's just what I like. Understand?"

"You can always find an answer, sweetheart," said Raymond, and he leaned over and kissed her firmly on the lips.

"Watch out," Jean whispered. "They rated you `mannerly and respectable'. While you have the wool over their eyes, you'd better keep it there. Because, brother, I know you better. You're a wolf," she laughed, "in sheep's clothing."

"Have your fun, sweetheart. You're at home and I can't retaliate. I'll get you later and you can put your foot on that."

From that point on, Raymond visited Jean's home often. Her father began to take for granted that the youngsters would eventually marry and began talking about how he could utilize Raymond's business skills in his large business. On Saturdays, when Raymond was spending the weekend in Natchez, he had always helped in the business. His willingness to work, and work for nothing, soon won the old man as his outspoken supporter. Papa Gravier would always give him a dollar or two for his services even though Raymond offered his services free.

Of all the joyous weekends in Natchez, Raymond remembered best Valentine's Day weekend in 1940. He and Jean had gone to a movie. They had observed some unbridled love scenes which stimulated them subtly to imitate the movie romance. On the way home, they stopped and kissed fervently at every dark or shadowy place on the street.

Raymond asked, "Isn't there a long way home? What about walking around the cemetery and coming up near your house? Can't we get through there?"

"Yes," said Jean. "We could see more moonlight, couldn't we?"

"Yes," said Raymond. So, arm in arm, they walked on toward the darker side of the cemetery.

This was a well-kept white cemetery which was partially enclosed by a small wall. As they walked into the darkness, the kisses became more frequent, more intimate and much longer. It was perfectly quiet—so quiet that Raymond said jokingly, "Nobody over here but you and me. You can't hear a ghost walking." At a very dark spot, made so by the shadow of a huge moss-covered oak, they stopped in front of a gate. Leaning against the gate feverishly kissing, they inadvertently pushed open the unlocked gate. "It said, `come in'," said Raymond. "Let's go over by that tree there and sit and talk. I'm not cold 'cause I got my love to keep me warm."

"No, I'm not cold, but I just don't think it's right. Furthermore, I'm scared," said Jean.

"I must show you, darling, that there is no such thing as a ghost." And with those words he picked Jean up in his arms, pushed the gate open, and did not stop until he reached the tree. Jean kicked a few times and feebly asked him to put her down, but Raymond knew she did not mean it. Upon reaching the tree about thirty yards from the gate, he put her down. Jean, sensing an increase in tempo, was very nervous. Raymond kissed her several times and took off his overcoat and threw it on the ground.

"What are you going to do?" Jean asked naively.

"Oh, we're going to sit here on my coat and talk for a few minutes."

It is not likely that Jean believed one word of it, but she sat down with Raymond. Without saying a word, he slipped his arm around her waist and began kissing her. He pushed her backward until both were lying on the overcoat. The ground was not cold to them. They were too occupied with themselves to feel it. When Raymond began removing Jean's clothing, she offered little resistance. Ready to give herself to him, she awaited his next move. So Raymond and Jean shared life-giving ecstasy in a place reserved for the dead.

As they left the cemetery, Raymond paused to close the gate. It gave a loud screech as if to say good-bye. Arm in arm, he and Jean walked toward home not saying a word—perhaps both were suffering from feelings of guilt. They had not walked far when Raymond noticed that Jean was crying. "What's the matter, honey?" said Raymond. "Are you angry, sweetheart? Tell me."

"No, I am not angry, I just feel so ashamed. I had promised my mother, myself, and my God that I would not know a man until my wedding night and now that dream is gone. If we ever get married, I'll be just another girl you've had."

"Stop crying, darling. You'll never be just another girl to me. You'll be my wife one day and every day will be a honeymoon with us. Really, I'm more in love with you now than I ever was because you have shown me that you are for me, body and soul. Now I have so much more to love you for. Doesn't that make sense?"

"Maybe so," said Jean, "when you look at it from your point of view, but that's not the way a respectable girl thinks. She wants to remain pure until she's married. Then there's something else to think about. Suppose I'm pregnant?"

"Now don't start worrying about that," said Raymond. "It's possible, but highly improbable. You remember what Doctor Sims said in our health education class? A woman can get pregnant only about seventy-two hours out of a month. Fate just wouldn't have it that you would get caught with those kind of odds on the very first time."

"It would be just my rotten luck and I'm scared already. I'd die if I were to come up p.g. I can just see my father going into a rage. I just can't be, can't be."

Raymond tried to joke with Jean. "You said, p.g., and old Doc Sims said college folk shouldn't use slang. I'll have to report that to him if you keep it up."

"This is no time for play. I'm dead serious and scared. What if I do have a baby?"

"I'd marry you, sweets, before you could say Jack Rabbit, and Mom and Pop couldn't argue long. Then, maybe I am sterile or you are barren and can't have children. Who knows?"

"Oh! Let me tell you something funny that happened in health education yesterday when you were absent. Doc was talking about the testes, the prostate glands and the male sex organs in general when the girl in the back corner who asks so many questions spoke up. She didn't know the scientific term and, as usual, Doc insisted that she call it by the name she knew. So she started her question: `Doctor Sims, if a man doesn't have any—you know—he can't get a baby, can he?' Doc said, 'For heaven's sake, say what you mean, I don't know what you mean by 'you know.'"

Raymond continued his story. "She tried again . . . 'If a man doesn't have any, any, any nuts.' The whole classroom went into an uproar, but Doc stood there with a stiff poker face and didn't crack a smile. He insisted that the embarrassment and the traumatic shock that one suffers in a case like that would permanently imprint the right scientific term in one's vocabulary. He went into a long exposition on the inability of black people to go to the doctor and indicate intelligently the ailment or place they feel pain. Doc told the class they must learn the scientific terms if for no other reason than to avoid pointing at certain places on the body when seeking professional advice. Comical as it was, Doc took that chance to teach a good lesson and drive some real points home."

"I know she felt like a plucked chicken," said Jean. "I can sympathize with her. Personally, I don't like that one thing about Doc Sims' teaching. He forces the students to use vulgarity—even when they don't want to. There must be a better way than that."

****

Raymond's moments of reflection were interrupted by Ida, the student nurse, who came in to bring the juice for the evening and to see that all was well before the lights were turned out. She then left Raymond to his thoughts, his pain, and his loneliness. As she left, she called out, "If you need me, just ring the bell and I'll come pronto."

When the spirit is low and when one is alone, it becomes a most difficult task to think positively. The quiet solitude of

130

night often turns optimism into pessimism, hope into despair, and dreams into temples already destroyed. In irrational reflection, one sometimes loses the will to live and toys with the idea of suicide.

Raymond could not easily forget his obsession with self-destruction. He wondered if it would not be better if he took one great leap to end it all. He concluded that death is not the worst thing in the world that could happen to a man, only the last. Man is not the creator of life—at no single moment can he say how long it will last. He lives for the minute, hoping that somehow the minutes will become hours, the hours days, and the days years. He tried to tell himself that life was not a process of continuous happiness, but an uneven mixture of misery, heartbreak and happiness.

In time of crisis, the negative or pessimistic aspects of life tend to be magnified. Solace can be found in only two ways— by looking backward in joyous remembrance on beauties of past life or by looking forward to the promises of the future, even the hereafter. Because Raymond possessed a past that he cherished, he was prevented from taking any drastic step during his midnight soul-searching. Immersed in beautiful memories of his time with Jean, he fell soundly asleep.

Chapter VIII

After thirty-four days, Raymond's face and hands were showing signs of healing. Although his normally dark brown face was white as a result of the burn and his left hand showed little sign of life, the doctor and Ida repeatedly assured him that he had much to be thankful for—that he had so much to live for. Of course, Raymond wanted to believe them, but when he looked at his charred hand doubled up in a fist, he knew that his case was worse than the doctor would admit. Would it not be better to die, he thought, than to live with a disfigured body? But always the will to live dominated.

The last day before leaving, Raymond was extremely remorseful. While he had learned to live with the difficulties of hospital life, he was deathly afraid to face the realities of the outside world. He dreaded the thought of going back to his rural community where the sin of being caught in a dance-hall fire was considered worse than adultery. He knew that the self-righteous members of the community would exact their pound of flesh, and he was not ready to pay that price. The thought of his homecoming filled him with great anxiety and he sought comfort in being alone. Most of his day was spent in meditation and self-condemnation.

Raymond retired to his bed, painfully aware that this would be his last night to sleep in his hospital bed. He knew he would miss Ida, the girl who knew exactly how to cheer him up whenever he was at his lowest ebb. Raymond knew that Ida loved him and would go to any lengths to prove it, but somehow the memory of Jean prevented him from being able to love Ida in return. He needed Ida—God! How he needed her! But need does not mean love. It was only Jean whom he loved, but Jean was dead.

Lying in bed after supper, tears streaming down his cheeks, his masculine pride made him hope that Ida would not come in and catch him crying. Ida walked in at the height of one of his emotional outbursts. Raymond hastily tried to dry his tears on the corner of the sheet. Ida did not go directly to the bed, but said from the door, "Cheer up, young man, because I'm going to give you a massage to make you remember this old hospital forever."

Raymond answered, "Not tonight, Ida. I think I've had enough exercise for today."

"Ah! There you go again," said Ida, "trying to tell the nurse what to do. As long as you're my patient, you'll do what I tell you to do until the last minute before you check out. Understand?"

"Okay, Ida, you win. I was just trying to save you a little work today."

Raymond was required to take therapy each day, but Ida had always made the therapy a little more pleasant by giving him an extra massage. At first, he thought the massage was part of the therapy, but later learned that the massage was Ida's own prescription. He had noticed the care and warmth with which she ran her hands gently over those parts of his body which were not burned, but he tried not to attach any deep significance to her efforts.

On this night, the doctor and the registered nurse had gone to a campus meeting and Ida and another practical nurse were the only staff members at the hospital. Ida gave Raymond the regular therapy and then began with her massage. Lying on his side in order not to irritate his back, Raymond felt Ida's hands move sensuously from his shoulders across his chest, to his navel, and then to his hips. Standing behind him, Ida rubbed his hips and hesitated for a minute as if deciding whether to continue. Her hands moved then to the front of his body. Both of Raymond's hands were bound in gauze and his back was extremely sore, but Ida made him forget his misery. Without saying a word, she kissed his charred lips, stripped off her panties and crawled into the narrow bed. Raymond did not need any hands because Ida carefully guided him. For the next few minutes, both were occupied with doing what comes naturally. Ida muffled Raymond's cries with kisses.

They lay in silence a few minutes later until Ida said, "Love me, Raymond?" Raymond mumbled something inaudible, but Ida didn't press him for an answer. Perhaps she felt that any act of love that could be so mutually satisfying on the first occasion had to have love as its base. She said, "I must clean up before the doctor returns." She put on her panties, took a washcloth and dampened it in the basin and gently washed Raymond's lower body with the same strokes she had used in the massage. She covered him with the sheet and tucked him in, gazed lovingly on his white face for a moment, patted both of his feet, and quietly left the room.

Chapter IX

The trip from Sweethill College to Corapeake was a rough one, both physically and emotionally. The gravel road was as bumpy as a country washboard, especially after rain. As Raymond sat in the 1936 Ford winding through the trees and canopy road called the Natchez Trace, he experienced the same kind of roughness and unsteadiness inside. In fact, he was scared to go home. For this time it would not be "home, sweet home," but a place of sharp eyes, loose tongues, and condemnation. While his father, mother, sister and brothers had apparently accepted his misfortune as a *fait accompli*, he wondered about their real feelings. Raymond felt like a prisoner being prepared for a slow social execution.

When Mr. and Mrs. Miles stopped on the black side of town to pick up a few things at the store, people ran to the car to speak to Raymond. Not for a minute did he believe that any of them were sincere. They were all curiosity seekers. As his father opened the door, people rushed up asking, "Ray, how are you doing?" He answered, "All right," even though he was dying inside.

Aunt Classy, a Bible-toting fundamentalist, greeted him and in the same breath asked: "Have you learned your lesson about staying out of dance halls, those dens of iniquity?" When Raymond didn't respond, she said: "Did you hear me, boy? Didn't they teach you at college that you must confess your sins before God and man, otherwise you are bound for hell and everlasting damnation will be your portion?"

Mother Miles, sensing Raymond's frustration, stepped between him and Aunt Classy and gently closed the car door. As they drove home, Raymond thought to himself, "I'll never go back to Corapeake again. Some of those self-righteous son-of-a-bitches looked like they were happy to see me like this."

For several weeks Raymond stayed at home with friends and relatives coming by to see him. At his parents' urging, he finally decided that he would go to Sunday School and church the next Sunday. But on Saturday morning, Papa Miles came into his room and said: "Son, the church council voted that because of your sins in a public place—a dance hall—you are no longer a member of the church. All you have to do is to appear before the church council at 4:00 p.m. today and tell them that you are sorry for your sins and ask for the church's forgiveness and for reinstatement." Raymond agreed to do it.

The church council was a socially cruel inquisition led by seven old men of the church, most often convened when young unmarried girls became pregnant. The poor unfortunate girl would stand crying and confessing her sins, but never did the council see fit to bring forth the father. Uncle Timothy Miles was one of the great inquisitors. Yet everybody knew that he was a "ladies' man who was known to whip up on them" on occasion, even his wife. In fact, a few weeks before the community had been buzzing with gossip that he had whipped

136

his wife, Aunt Leola, because she accepted a soda pop from Deacon Tyson. According to the council's policies, public drunkenness and wife-beating were offenses which called for immediate expulsion from the church. So just before the council was to meet Raymond called his father aside and said to him: "Papa, I'm going to confess my sins like you told me, but I'm going to publicly insist that the council require Uncle Timothy to confess his sins for whipping Aunt Leola three weeks ago. I want you to know that I respect you, Papa, but it's nothing you can do to keep me from saying this." Papa Miles warned, "Don't you do that, boy. You don't save your soul by destroying someone else's. Do you hear me, boy?" "Yes, Papa," said Raymond. "But I must insist that Uncle Timothy confess if I have to confess."

At four o'clock the council was convened and it turned out to be a stormy meeting. Being brought before the council was a short, black, big-hipped, moronic woman who was pregnant with her first child at the age of twenty-eight. Ceily, who didn't know how to say "no," had often been caught behind the barn or even the church by many of the male members of the church from the time she was twelve years old. A couple of deacons joked that they never knew Ceily was capable of having a baby. But Ceily's inquisition turned out to be anything but a laughing matter. When they called for her confession and plea for forgiveness, Ceily stood up and said, "Yes, I did wrong. And I know that my God will forgive me. But all of you are just as guilty as I am. Nobody out there can throw a stone at me." Then she began to call the names of men in the church who had once "pulled down my drawers." At first, a dead silence fell over the council, and then the council chairman, Uncle Timothy, tried to shut her up and escort her out of the council.

But before they could get her out she yelled: "This baby belongs to old Deacon Smitty Andrews over there," pointing a finger at a staunch member of the council. "I was going across the field one day and old Smitty caught me, pulled off my drawers, and threw me under a gum tree and ravished me. If I'm telling a lie, God's a possum dog."

As they carried a yelling Ceily from the church, the council was adjourned with a shaky prayer for unity, and no mention was made of Raymond's ordeal in the dance-hall fire. Ceily's confession not only caused widespread gossip, but led to Smitty's divorce and brought an end to the meetings of the church council. Although everybody knew that Ceily was playing with a half deck both mentally and emotionally, her testimony carried a strange ring of truth which shocked the entire community.

Free from the shame of publicly confessing his sins, Raymond's recuperation at home was slow but steady. Although the brown color was returning to his white face and hands, he was still sensitive about going out. One day while he was at home brooding, Maude, a nearby neighbor's sister from Vicksburg who was visiting in the country, came over to the house to draw a pail of water from their deep well. After drawing the water she came to the door and called "Ray! I'm coming in." When she walked in Ray was surprised to see that she was no longer the spindly, flat-chested, tomboyish girl that he remembered from several years ago, but had fully rounded out in all of the right places. Not only had she grown physically, but she had developed a sexual aggressiveness that really shocked him.

With almost no conversation after greeting him, she walked over to the other side of the room where Ray was standing in his nightshirt, reached out and caught his white hands and held them for a moment. It appeared that she was going to cry. She softly placed one hand over his shoulder and moved in and caught him and pulled him to her as she laid her head on his chest. She directed his hand under her short dress. Within minutes, she was in Raymond's bed, giving him what she later called "the best treatment in the world for burns." For a week Maude returned for water at the same time—a time when she knew that everybody would be in the field picking cotton and Raymond would be at home alone. Although he knew that Maude was a girl he could never learn to love, he looked forward daily to receiving the "best treatment in the world for burns." But at the beginning of the next week, Maude went back to Vicksburg and Raymond never saw her again. When he heard from her sister that she had gone back home, Raymond thought to himself, "She left and never even thought to say good-bye. Maybe my bed work didn't make a good impression on her."

****

Everybody looked forward to Saturday in Corapeake— walking from one end of the street to the other, meeting people, showing off new clothes, or just "hanging out." It was a day for socializing, buying a soda pop and a buffalo fish or catfish sandwich, and for some, getting juiced up on a few shots of bootleg liquor or moonshine. Describing the good time that black people had on Saturday night, people used to say, "If a white man could be black for just one Saturday night in a saw-mill town, he'd never go back to his people again."

But a month had passed and Raymond had not been to town. His sensitivity about his burns caused him to avoid meeting people. It was hard enough to go to church. But this

Saturday Evella and several of his friends encouraged him to come to town. In town, Raymond sat in the car for a long time refusing to walk until Evella dragged him out of the car and forced him to walk all over town with her. Of course, black people walked very carefully and talked quietly as they walked to the post office on the white side of town. Blacks could sit on the bench in front of the post office for a bit of rest or a little conversation, but if a white person came and sat down on the other end, the black person knew to get up immediately. As Raymond and Evella entered the post office, he saw something on the bulletin board that was to change his life forever. He saw a sign which said: "Colored boys between 17 and 25 wanted as mess boys in the U.S. Navy." Raymond took down the address carefully because he felt that this might be his passport out of Corapeake. Away from eyes that condemn and pass judgment, to a new beginning in an outfit that promised him he could see the world—a new beginning that would lead to greater personal freedom and independence.

Led back to the black side to town, across the railroad track which separated whites from blacks, Raymond was scarcely aware that Evella was holding his hand. He was thinking about a career in the Navy. While he knew full well that mess boys were nothing but flunkies catering to white men's needs, he would try anything that would take him out of Corapeake.

On the black side of the track there were large stacks of pulpwood and railroad crossties alongside the tracks which, near sundown, cast a shadow on the stores, funeral home, cafes, barber shops, beauty parlors, and juke joints which made up what some people derisively called "frog town." In front of these businesses were long plank benches crowded with jovial people gossiping, raising hell and just enjoying a normal Saturday evening in town. From the largest juke joint, a place called Blueberry Hill, which many Christians had condemned and tried to get the sheriff to close, one could hear racially degrading music blasting loudly enough to be heard across the track on the white side of town. One of the songs which appeared to be a favorite was called "Bottle'Em up and Go." Raymond cringed when he saw the white police smiling at one of the song's most detestable verses:

> The nigger and the white man
> Playing seven-up
> The nigger beat the white man
> And was scared to pick it up.
> He had to bottle 'em up and go.

Black men and women danced to the sultry but degrading music in a place that was a small replica of the Rhythm Club in Natchez. The windows were boarded up with only a front door entrance and exit. Like the Rhythm Club, Blueberry Hill reflected a society where the dominant white race had forced black people to accept a notion of racial inferiority and second-class citizenship. Hence blacks could dance, sing and enjoy themselves to the degrading song "Bottle 'Em Up and Go." As children walked the streets and heard their elders singing its lyrics, they were learning that this was a white man's world where they, like their elders, would eventually have to "bottle 'em up and go."

Black children could see daily the effects of white domination in a society which kept them in their places. Even elderly black men and women referred to white teenagers as "Mr." and "Miss," while white men and women referred to respected black teachers, preachers, deacons, or businessmen as "boy" or "girl." It was a closed society in which blacks had to be prepared to "bottle 'em up and go" in order to survive.

In a society so completely dominated by white oppression of blacks, black people frequently learn and practice self-hatred and openly denigrate their own blackness. So instead of black being beautiful, blackness was seen not as beautiful but as an ugly condition to be shunned. Any little boy or girl in Mississippi society knew: "If you're white, you're right; if you're brown, stick around; if you're black, get back." Just as the old blues song "Bottle 'Em Up and Go" denigrated the black man's courage and portrayed him as a coward, another popular record on the piccolo at that time reinforced in young and old alike that blackness was damnable. The degrading lyrics went:

> My mamma done told me
> When I was a little boy playing number peg;
> Don't drink no black cow's milk,
> Don't eat no black hen's egg.

Listening to the degrading song, Raymond considered the plight of black people and their apparent acceptance of the status quo. His mind took him back to the dastardly acts of Bulldog Johnson, the policeman who spent three-fourths of his time on the black side of town, making all his arrests among black people. He recalled one of his schoolmates' encounters with Bulldog. Like most of the other black boys who did not get away to college or to Chicago—the black Mississippian's paradise—Cepheus, Raymond's friend, went to work in the local sawmill, pulling lumber ten hours a day and a half day on Saturday for $1.25 per day. It was not long before he had abandoned all of the Christian teaching of Uncle Timothy Miles, his father, and had begun running with the sawmill crowd. As the African proverb states, "If you run with wolves, you will learn to howl." The young Cepheus had certainly learned to howl. He drank, gambled, and chased women with the best of them. And because he was so good-looking, he had women chasing him from all sides, and all of them knew that he was not hard to catch. In gambling, he was good with dice, but better with "Three Card Molly." He was known to take a sucker's money in a minute. When Bulldog had caught Cepheus gambling and arrested him a few months before, he had told Cepheus that in exchange for 25 percent of his winnings, he would never arrest him again. Cepheus refused, with dire consequences.

One Saturday sometime later, suckers gathered around the bench on the back side of the Blueberry Hill juke joint. Cepheus called out, "You! You, sucker! Find the red card. Four bits to two bits you can't." He showed the three cards, two black and one red, and with sleight of hand, beat one gullible man after another out of his hard-earned cash. Just as the game was getting into high gear with plenty of money on the bench, old Bulldog Johnson, the white policeman, came out of nowhere and said, "I got you smart-ass niggers now. Leave every goddam penny on the bench and put your black hands in the air." Quick as a flash, Cepheus grabbed up the money and began running toward the water tower. Bulldog ran after him for a few paces, then dropped to one knee, and using his left arm to steady his aim, fired three shots in rapid succession at Cepheus. Cepheus stumbled forward, started reeling and fell into the doorway of the town's creamery. For a moment everybody stood stunned. Then somebody yelled: "Hell, man! you didn't have to shoot him. He ain't done nothing to you. Why did you shoot him? Why did you shoot him, man?" All the time the blacks were moving toward Bulldog, who still had his gun in his hand. The fear was beginning to show on his red face as he backed away slowly. Then Bulldog spoke:

"Now it ain't no need for any more of you niggers to get shot. You better get down the hill and see about that lawbreaker. I didn't break the law, that nigger Cepheus broke the law. All of you broke the law." Although Bulldog was talking tough, he looked scared. He forgot about the money which he usually tried to take during gambling arrests, and he forgot about the people who were gambling with Cepheus. He headed back across the track and later returned with four armed white men, members of the town's so-called Sheriff's Posse.

In the meantime, some of Cepheus's friends were attending to him as he lay breathing hard in the creamery doorway. He had taken a bullet in the shoulder. He was in terrific pain, but still conscious, moaning, "That big-bellied bastard didn't have to shoot me. He didn't have to shoot me." He passed out as his friends put him into the car and sped down the rocky road toward the hospital. They rushed him into the emergency room, only to be told that he must be carried back to the side marked "Colored Only." In the segregated hospital, the doctors performed surgery only after finding out who was going to "pay for this boy." After his recuperation, Cepheus, like so many blacks before him, realized that he could not live in Corapeake. Within a month of his recovery, Cepheus caught the "Bee," a train that would take him to Chicago, a promised land where a man could be a man. The day after the shooting, Bulldog was patrolling the black side of town as if nothing had happened. The black folks said, "He's over here just looking for another nigger to shoot."

Wherever oppression and racial discrimination exist, it is painful to live from day to day, but sometimes it is even more painful to look back. Remembering the story of Cepheus brought to Raymond's mind an even more sordid and painful blot on Mississippi's racial history. He remembered that when
144

he was in eleventh grade at the Training School in Corapeake, one of the best football players, J.C. Franklin, had been lynched by a white mob. J.C. was a handsome chap who took pride in his well-developed body. He would brag that he had a body to rival that of the bodybuilder Charles Atlas. He was a dark brown man with large shoulders, a neat waist, muscular calves and thighs, long curly hair and a smile that could immediately win and influence people. Attending the nearby white school, but living within three blocks of the black school, was Judy Cameron, a tall and buxom girl with long auburn hair, known around town to be mentally and emotionally off. Judy may not have known many things, but she did know that she was in love with J.C. Franklin. From the very beginning to the end, she wrote him a letter every day. Somewhere along the line, they violated the South's strictest taboo—a white girl and a black boy fell in love. From time to time, they would meet and make love on cardboard boxes underneath the black training school which was built on the side of a hill. Blacks had known for several months what was going on and some had advised J.C. of the chance that he was taking. In fact, people thought that Mr. Cameron knew too, because he liked J.C. and let him work around the store from time to time.

One day when J.C. and Judy were at their secret rendez-vous, a truckload of white ruffians escorted by Bulldog Johnson caught them in the act under the school. They let the crying girl go amid screams of "I love him, I love him." But they whipped the naked J.C. mercilessly. They would have killed him on the spot, but Bulldog convinced them not to do so. For his own protection, J.C. was placed in the county jail and charged with the rape of a white woman.

The white public defender tried to get J.C. to plead guilty. In jail, he was beaten, threatened with castration, placed in

145

solitary confinement, and denied food, but J.C. would never confess to rape. He maintained that they were lovers. He even had his mother gather as evidence the daily letters that Judy had written declaring her love for him and describing their lovemaking. One of the letters read:

J.C., My Love,

I am writing you today as always to tell you how much I love you. Yesterday, when I was in your arms, I felt just like I was in heaven. The darkness under the school felt like our own little home, with you and me all alone. Regardless of what they say, you are my husband and I am your wife. And it will always be that way. The only time that I feel like somebody is when I'm with you.

You know that I love you with all my heart. I love the way you make me feel. You are so strong and feel so big and long inside of me. But you are very gentle and sweet to me. Sometimes you hurt me just a little bit, but as I told you, "it hurts so good." I wish that I could be with you every day, but I know that is too dangerous. But as you said, we could go on forever if we are careful. Or maybe, you'll have to go to Chicago and let me join you there.

I get so tired of people saying that I'm crazy. You know that I'm not crazy, except I may be a little crazy over you. I'm a real good student in school when I want to be. Whenever I make love to you, I am so relaxed and feel so complete. I can come home and study my lessons and make good grades in all my classes. If you could just go to my school or I to your school, we both might be geniuses. (smile) Sweetheart, don't ever doubt my love. I've never had any man in the world but you. And you know what? I don't ever want anyone else. But I'm also jealous. I don't want you looking around at those cute colored girls over at your school. Save all your love and strength for me for next Thursday. You will need it because I'll be ready to give you all the love I've got. Please love me always, hun, because I could not live a day without your love.

My love always,

Judy

Judy wrote the judge several letters telling him that she and J.C. were lovers. However, white men in Corapeake and throughout the South believed that white women cannot love black men. In their view, no evidence of any kind could exonerate J.C. Thus, the letters were banned from the courtroom and ordered destroyed. Judy was to be placed in an asylum for the insane.

Somehow the news got out that J.C. would be freed if Judy's letters could be admitted as evidence in a court of appeal. The news of J.C.'s possible appeal and the chance that he might be freed inspired a mob led by well-known Klan members to storm the jail one Saturday night, take J.C. out on the upper Homochitto River, castrate him, and hang him from the limb of a large oak tree. A note left at the scene of the lynching advised, "Let this be a lesson to all Coons."

No one was ever even accused of J.C.'s murder. When news reached town of J.C.'s death, Judy, who was to be taken to the insane asylum at Whitfield that Monday, found her father's 12-gauge shotgun, put it in her mouth, and pulled the trigger. Two lives had been senselessly sacrificed in the name of racial segregation.

Raymond knew that Corapeake was no place for him. It was a place that was depressing to the spirit and detrimental to the soul of black folks. Corapeake was no place for black people to live, especially a proud, half-educated black man. One step out of line and he, like J.C., would be `strange fruit' hanging from a tree. Raymond remembered that just after J.C.'s lynching, he and his mother were in the railroad station buying a ticket to visit Grandma. A white ticket saleslady at the station reached over and felt his curly hair. His mother exploded, "Don't you ever put your hands on my boy again.

Never! Never! Never! Just don't you touch him." The white woman stood there in silence for she, too, knew that she had violated the very first lesson in southern etiquette for white women—never touch a black male affectionately, regardless of his age.

When they walked out of the station, Raymond asked: "Mama, why did you get so angry? The woman didn't do anything." His mother then gave him a lesson in race relations that every successful black mother had learned—a lesson that enabled them to protect their sons from the wrath of the Ku Klux Klan and the lynch mobs.

"Raymond, baby, there are only two free groups of people in the South—white men and black women. White women and black men are social slaves—their lives are totally controlled by white men. White men and black women have been going together for years and in that respect they have been free. Everybody knows it; nobody says anything. But let a high-class Christian boy like you just look at some of that `po white trash,' smelling just like a peckerwood, and he becomes mob bait. Just, look at what happened to J.C.—a boy who was lynched for absolutely nothing."

"On the other hand," she continued, "You take that no-good black gal, Doodle Cates. She's been going with old Bulldog Johnson ever since she was thirteen years old. All the town knew it but it made no difference. He built that nice little bungalow house that she lives in and gave her those two little white boys that she drags around with her. He's down there every night, eating, sleeping and doing everything else that he's big enough to do. But the good people in town don't say a word about racial segregation. Not even when he whipped Doodle for sleeping with a big black millhand nigger named Jumbo

Green. He whipped her so bad that he put her in the hospital. Even while she was in the hospital, Bulldog visited her and held her hand. They tell me she was lying there grinning just like nothing had happened."

Mama Miles was warming to her subject. "But one time, Doodle put a whipping on Bulldog down by the McNeil Store. She was talking with a group of Negroes and apparently Bulldog wanted to see her. So he grabbed her arm and started dragging her toward his car. You know that she was a short woman with a big butt built close to the ground. She was all over him like white on rice, slapping, hitting, and cussing like a sailor. She even knocked his gun out of its holster. That was the funniest thing that I've ever seen in my life. Nothing ever came out of it but black folks talked. They say white men love black women by night and hate them by day. But old Bulldog must love Doodle all the time, because he's been with her since she was thirteen."

Mama Miles concluded, "So Raymond, baby, it's a double standard in Corapeake. But when they chased your brother Hosie out of town thirteen years ago, I said to myself that if white men ever tried to mess with either of my boys that are left, they'll get them over my dead body. I mean it and I'm ready to die to protect my family. Getting mad with those fresh white women who are trying to flirt with you is my way of protecting you from temptation. I've told you all this because I want you to understand the way things are."

Raymond understood his mother's concern and how much she loved him and wanted to protect him. But since black teachers, preachers, businessmen and all upstanding blacks had to submit to even the most ignorant white trash, it seemed to Raymond that he could never make the proper adjustment in

Corapeake. He knew that he had a place that was assigned to him by the white race, but he was not sure that he could stay in his place. For his sake and for his mother's sake he had to get out of Corapeake. Maybe, just maybe, the Navy would lead Raymond from his enslavement in "Egypt's land" across the seas into a land of promise—a land of greater freedom.

In three weeks at home, Raymond had made remarkable progress in overcoming many of his problems. His hands had just about straightened out and the proper color was returning to his face and hands. The local doctor said that he had never seen a burn heal so smoothly and quickly. In addition to the prescribed medicine that the doctor had given him, he also used Grandma's remedy, soaking his hands and washing his face several times a day in elderberry juice. Grandma said that this was the best way to bring back his color after the burn. The combination of treatments worked miracles for Raymond.

Each day he would walk two hundred yards up the path to the mailbox hoping to get a letter from the U.S. Navy. The application he had filled out indicated it would take three or four weeks to get an answer, but he started going to the mailbox the very first week.

At first, he received little support from his family about a career in the Navy. The stereotype of worldly, hard-drinking, women-chasing infidels was something that did not sit well with his Christian family. Papa Miles would say: "The Navy is no place for a Christian boy. It'll take you to Sodom and Gomorrah where wickedness will consume you. That Natchez thing should have taught you that you are prone to yield to temptation; that you are weak in the flesh. So stay here, boy, get your soul right with the Lord, and marry Darline who is a God-fearing girl who was brought up glorifying God. Get yourself a teaching job, and stay in your place. You'll find that Corapeake is a good place to live because it has some fine white folks who respect niggers. Take me. I can walk in the bank and borrow $200 on my own signature and I don't have but a fourth-grade education. I know my place and everybody respects me."

Papa Miles continued, "It's only when we sin—when we go out seeking strange flesh, worldly things—that God brings us back down to size. The Natchez fire taught you that, and believe me when I tell you, `the wages of sin is death.' The Navy was made by the devil for his people. Don't become one of them."

Raymond knew that there was no need to talk back to Papa Miles. He held to his position in an argument as tenaciously as a pit bulldog. The only person who could change him was Mama Miles, so Raymond begged her to make his father consent to let him go. A couple of weeks later at Sunday breakfast with all gathered around the table as usual, Papa Miles prayed his long prayer. He prayed for his family, the community, the church, the government (teach them to love and respect all people) and, strangely enough, for the Navy—a Christian Navy. As Raymond listened, he recognized that somehow Mama Miles had gotten to him. He was now free to go into the Navy.

Less than two weeks later, a letter came to Raymond from the Bureau of Navigation, the agency of government under which the U.S. Navy operated at that time. He nervously opened the letter and read the orders to report to the Federal Building in New Orleans on October 24, 1940. Raymond's heart leaped for joy. This was his passport out of Corapeake. The letter told him what to bring, where to live in New Orleans, and what to expect by way of medical examination. He was told that colored boys had to be well-developed and suitable to serve in an officers' mess. As he looked at his hands and face which still showed visible signs of the burns, he wondered if he would ever pass the physical examination. He wasn't certain, but he knew one thing. He had to try.

Just as they had done when he decided to go to Sweethill College, his sister, church members and former classmates gave him a going-away party at the church. There were games, plenty of food, and merrymaking for everyone. Raymond enjoyed the party and thanked his well-wishers, but doubts filled his mind. What if I mess up in the Navy like I did in school? What will I say if the Navy rejects me and I have to come back home? Will I yield to temptation like my father said? Should I leave home or should I just stay here and teach?

The day before he was to report, Raymond stood at the railroad station where black people always stood, waiting for the Bee. Instead of going north to Chicago like most of his friends, he was going south to New Orleans. They all had one thing in common—trying to get out of Corapeake and out of Mississippi. They were all searching for freedom, but only time would tell if they would find it.

Chapter X

The Bee moved rapidly down the track through the rural countryside toward New Orleans, the Crescent City. It was only a few miles from Corapeake to the Louisiana line, but Raymond had been in the state only once, when a group from his high school attended a football game at Southern University. He had ridden the train several times before, going to Grandma's house and to Sweethill College, but never such a great distance. It would be a joy to ride a train such a long way, especially when the U.S. Navy was paying for it. So he sat excitedly by the window counting telephone poles, cars, and livestock as he passed. Whenever he came to a small town and saw black people standing in the 'colored' section at the station, he would wave and they would wave back just as if they knew him. In a general way, he was happy as he watched the world go by. Most of all, he was happy because he was leaving Corapeake behind.

Mississippi and Louisiana were essentially alike in their treatment of blacks, both enforcing strict segregation. Raymond was forced to sit in a coach marked "for colored only." Since most trains had coal-burning engines which threw off blasts of smoke, black people were required to sit in the first coach behind the engine. Since there was no air conditioning, windows had to remain open on warm days, and blacks would inhale most of the smoke that came in through the open windows. Also, they would be more painfully exposed to the piercing sounds of whistles blowing as the train approached every cow path that crossed the tracks. Raymond also waved out of the window at black folks whom he saw picking the last bits of cotton, cutting the sugar cane, or picking truck crops that were in season. He thought, "Black folks are the same almost everywhere in the South. If there's cotton to be picked, cane to be cut, pulpwood to be loaded or manual labor to be done, you'll find them there. White people are living off the sweat of black people's brows." He hoped that he was getting away from it all, but he recognized the contradictions in his thinking. He was going to a Navy where he could be only a messboy. He knew that regardless of how high he got in the Messmen's Branch of the Navy, he would always be a servant, a hash slinger, a drawer of water and a hewer of wood for the white man. Though he was voluntarily offering himself for service in the U.S. Navy, he wondered if he would forever be a servant, or would one day be free to be a man among men.

Raymond looked at the sights as he traveled and compared them with his own hometown and state. As the train went through Jackson, Louisiana, he saw the Louisiana State Mental Hospital and remembered poor Judy Cameron, who had blown her brains out rather than go to the mental hospital after her lover was lynched. If the Louisiana hospital is anything like they say it was at Whitfield in Jackson, Mississippi, he mused, if you are not crazy when you get there, it won't be long before you will be. These are places where people who merely fail to conform to social patterns or who do not measure up to Southern stereotypes are thrown on the scrap heap, and nobody seems to care.

At the same junction, he also saw a sign pointing toward Angola, the Louisiana State Penitentiary. With populations less than half black, both Louisiana and Mississippi had more than seventy-five percent of their maximum security prison cells filled with black men. He had heard black men argue over which was the most vile and brutal, Parchman State Prison in Mississippi or Angola in Louisiana. Most maintained that Angola had the edge since it was surrounded by swamplands infested with alligators. So when a black man escaped, if the white man couldn't catch him, the alligators would. Raymond thought of the prison and the asylum, two social institutions which affected black people's lives so frequently in so many incidents of injustice. He thought, how many black men have died because white people would not let themselves believe that a white woman could be in love with a black man? And how many white women have been driven stark mad because their lovers were lynched or imprisoned?

Is this a way of life, he thought, that the Army, Navy and Marines should protect? Yet he found himself volunteering for the Navy, a branch of the military that told him up front that he could only be a servant for the dominant race. In fact, the U.S. Navy was the most segregated branch of the armed forces. It did not recruit black men for service in any branch of the Navy between 1919 and 1932. And when it began taking messboys in 1932, it restricted applications to southern states where blacks were more likely to be docile and obedient.

The Bee puffed its way to the outskirts of Baton Rouge. Seven miles above Baton Rouge was the home of Leland College in the village of Baker. Leland College had trained the Reverend Jaggert, the minister who had preached the eulogy at the mass funerals in Natchez after the dance-hall fire. A Baptist-supported college with a reputation for turning out excellent teachers and preachers, Leland College had been a godsend for black people, providing black leadership long before the state of Louisiana began supporting its black college. Some people maintained that Leland was "Uncle Tom" in its orientation and accommodated the notion of white superiority for a few dollars in white donations. Regardless of its acceptance of the status quo in race relations, if Leland hadn't done anything else but graduate the likes of Jaggert, it would still have been a blessing to black people and to the South.

Over the flatlands of Louisiana with its cane fields, sugar mills, rice paddies and truck crops, the train followed closely the Mississippi River levee and causeways until it rolled into New Orleans. Raymond was astonished by the sheer size of the Union Station and by the hordes of people walking to and fro. He was relieved when he found his Aunt Lizzie waiting at the gate to take him to her home on Melpomene Street for the night. From his humanities class at Sweethill College, he remembered that Melpomene was the muse of tragedy. With all the tragedy that had befallen him in recent weeks, he could not help thinking that the street name was an ill omen.

Aunt Lizzie and Uncle Ozzie welcomed him with open arms, but their subsequent remarks increased his apprehension. Both were devout Jehovah's Witnesses who were bitterly opposed to military force. They told him that to prepare for war against other men was a sinful act which God himself condemns. The only battle for which we should be preparing is the battle of Armageddon, the final conflict between the forces of good and evil. Since God will be the Captain, good will prevail over evil and the world as we know it will then come to an end. Aunt Lizzie told Raymond emphatically: "Change your mind, boy, and go back home. Return to the God of your elders. You are seeking idol gods. You are entering a white man's navy to fight for a white man's way of life. Baal has always been the white man's god. He worships money and power. He will kill in a minute to keep everything he worships. So when you join up with a group like that, nothing good will ever come to you. Mind me when I tell you, boy, nothing good will ever come to you."

Raymond's background had taught him to respect older people. Thus, it was rather unnerving when Aunt Lizzie "put her mouth on him" by prophesying that evil would befall him. He wrestled with worries all night as he looked forward to his physical examination by the Navy on the following morning.

At eight o'clock the next morning, Uncle Ozzie and Aunt Lizzie dropped Raymond off at the Federal Building on Canal Street where he would take his physical exam. Upon leaving Aunt Lizzie said, "I can't wish you good luck, for God knows, I hope you fail." With these discouraging words they drove away and Raymond walked upstairs to await his uncertain future.

Raymond was taken by a guide to a room where eleven other black young men were waiting for their exams. To Raymond, they all looked strong and healthy—not an apparent blemish on their bodies. His face and hands still had small white splotches on them. "If they take only one out of every two volunteers," he thought, "I know that I don't have a chance with these splotches."

In the limited conversation in the waiting room, he learned that the twelve young men represented six southern states— Alabama, Florida, Georgia, Louisiana, Mississippi and South Carolina. He had been told that in selecting the final recruits, white officers would be concerned with the courtesy and deference the candidates showed to white men. He was determined that if his burns did not disqualify him, he would say "Yes Sir," "No Sir," scratch his head, and do all the things Uncle Tom did to fool white people. He could not go back to Corapeake a failure again.

Raymond passed the physical exam with flying colors. The two questions asked by the doctors had little to do with his physical condition. They wanted to know, "How did you get burned like this? And why does a boy with a year in college want to join the Navy?" To the second question, Raymond would always answer that he wanted to see the world. He knew that if he had told them that he was running away from a conservative, oppressive, segregated social system where black men could be beaten, shot or lynched with impunity, he would not have been chosen as a messboy recruit.

When Raymond was called in for personal counseling, he noticed on the doctor's recommendation: "A well-developed, normal colored boy with burn splotches on his face and hands. Color should be restored within six weeks. Should develop into a good and responsible messboy." After a short explanation, Raymond arose to leave the office to join the other boys in the waiting room. He was a little surprised when the doctor stopped him and asked: "Are you sure you'd rather be a messboy in the Navy than a teacher of agriculture in Corapeake?" Raymond interpreted this as a question growing out of a sense of guilt for putting a highly trained person in

158

the Messmen's Branch. Nevertheless he answered, "I plan to save my money and finish college later."

Seven out of twelve volunteers were accepted and Raymond was among them. Although the announcement had advertised for four-year terms of enlistment, the officer who gave them the Oath of Loyalty told them that they were enlisting for six-year terms. Nobody objected and all were sworn in for six-year terms of service in the Messmen's Branch of the Navy.

The new recruits were told that they would spend the night at the Astoria Hotel on Rampart Street and leave for Norfolk, Virginia the next morning. The petty officer gave the black recruits a stern lecture upon dismissing them for the hotel. "Boys, you're in the Navy now. You people know that from now on your ass belongs to the Navy. So keep it clean. When you get over to the Astoria this evening, you'll find whores all over the place. But let me tell you something. Just keep your dick in your pants; I don't give a damn how good the whore looks, just stay away from her. If you show up in Norfolk with the claps or the pox, they'll throw your ass in the brig—jail. Remember, get your dinner, go to bed, and keep your ass clean and hang on to your orders. See you boys tomorrow morning. Say, 'aye, aye, Sir.'"

Rampart Street was a center of inner city black life. There were small stores, taverns, juke joints, jazz bands, open-air fruit and vegetable markets, street vendors, barber shops, salons, and restaurants proudly advertising "red beans and white rice." The Astoria Hotel was perhaps the best hotel in the central city. It was known for its gumbo and crayfish bisque, comfortable rooms—and call girls. Everybody who visited the Astoria Hotel would remember it for one reason or another.

When Raymond and the other six recruits entered the Astoria Hotel and walked to the second floor, three shapely, scantily clad Creole girls were standing near the doorway smiling. Finally, one girl raised her short dress to her waist and said, "If you boys want some of this, get your dollars out and follow me. I'll give you something you'll never forget."

None of the boys responded but kept on to their rooms. Some of the boys were too young and scared to think about an evening with a call girl, and the lecture by the petty officer at the examination station was still ringing in their ears. "Keep your ass clean...they'll throw your ass in the brig." So they came downstairs and ate as a group and returned to their rooms until they were picked up and taken to the train station for the trip to Norfolk.

Like all trains in the South, the train was segregated with blacks in the front coach immediately behind the smokestack. As the train moved from Bristol, Tennessee toward Norfolk, large numbers of white soldiers boarded the train. When seats reserved for white people were filled, the conductor came to the coach "for colored only" and commanded all blacks to move up and fill all seats starting at the front, placing three passengers to the seat. When all were seated approximately half the coach was filled. To make certain that a partition was placed between the blacks and whites, as required by law, the black porter placed a string between the seats and hung several sheets from the Sunday comic strips to separate whites and blacks.

The black sailors and the other black people moved into the crowded space that the conductor assigned to them. No one offered a single strong protest. Raymond could see clearly the results of years of social control and social conditioning. Blacks paid the same fare as whites, but allowed their rights and privileges to be taken away without a word. Aunt Lizzie was right, he thought, when she told me that I was entering the Navy to "fight for the white man's way of life." He also remembered one of his professors at Sweethill saying: "Black people must become makers of symbols and images in our society if they expect to survive and prosper. For he who makes symbols and images controls minds; and he who controls minds has nothing to fear from bodies." It was obvious in that train coach that whites controlled blacks' minds.

Upon arriving in Norfolk they were met by a bus and taken to the Norfolk Naval Base and placed in segregated quarters called Unit B-East. All black messmen received their training at two makeshift sets of barracks called Unit K-West and Unit B-East. The barracks to which Raymond was assigned reminded him of the old Rhythm Club in Natchez. The first thing he did was to walk around a bit to find exits. He was glad to note that the windows were not barred as they had been in Natchez.

Chapter XI

Training of the black recruits was under the directorship of Steward First Class Ferguson who was proud of his 32 years in the Navy. He was a good and dutiful steward and he knew it. With a big belly and a gruff voice that got everyone's attention, he yelled out to the newly dressed and lined-up messboys: "You boys are here for one reason and only one reason—to learn how to be good mess attendants for the officers. So during the next eight weeks, I and my assistants will teach you everything you need to know. I'm proud of the fact that my mess attendants are known throughout the Navy as `Ferguson's Boys.' They are always neat, clean, courteous, punctual and willing to give service. My reputation in the Navy is on the line with each class and no little punk is going to destroy Steward Ferguson's reputation. Do you understand? Say,`aye, aye, Sir.'" The new mess attendants shouted, "aye, aye, Sir" in unison.

Steward Ferguson noticed Raymond's hands and face and decided not to assign him to food service details. Because he could type 40 words per minute, he was placed in the Glass House, the administration center, where he soon became the company clerk. However, during the eight weeks, Raymond went through all phases of boot training—swimming tests, drills, gas house and military maneuvers which taught one how to survive in war and peace. Most emphasis was placed on the social etiquette of dealing with officers, making beds and keeping the officers' quarters and preparing for serving the meals. Ferguson was a master teacher and soon had the 45 boys ready to graduate and be assigned to ships. Raymond emerged as the honor man in Class 5, and because of his typing skills, he was kept at Unit B-East for two additional months.

No one trained under Steward Ferguson could ever forget his lectures to mess attendants who were going on liberty in Norfolk for the very first time. To Raymond he sounded like Papa Miles when he was talking about sin in Natchez, but Steward Ferguson's language was more graphic.

You young bucks are going on liberty today for the first time. So I want every ass to listen to Steward Ferguson and take in every damn word he says. You are going to Norfolk— a city that is known throughout the Navy as 'shit city.' The main street in shit city is called Church Street. But believe me when I tell you that there ain't an ounce of religion on Church Street. It's a street that's filled with whores, pimps, punks (that's fairies) who are just waiting to screw up you young, country-ass sailors. So don't go to Norfolk thinking you can match wits with the street people. Leave some of your money at home, stay in groups, select a buddy who doesn't drink and do what he tells you to do. Don't miss your curfew! You hear, don't miss your curfew!

Now some of you think you got to get some tonight. My best advice is to keep that thing in your pants. If you can't, here are some condoms and some pro-kits for each of you to use. If you use these you have a ninety-percent chance of avoiding gonorrhea and syphilis. Now there is a good-looking gal on Church Street named Chow-Chow. Avoid her like the plague. She's sent more men to the sick bay than any woman in Norfolk. Avoid the Crescent Club because it's a den for punks. There's no place in the Navy for a sissy. I hate a sissy like I hate a skunk.

I might sound rough, but I see each of you as a green son of mine who thinks he knows everything but knows nothing. Norfolk is more than you can handle, boys. So stay sober, go in groups, use the rubbers and pro-kits, and be back here ready for reveille tomorrow. Men dismissed.

Raymond heeded Steward Ferguson's advice and avoided trouble in Norfolk. Church Street was indeed Sodom and Gomorrah at its best, but he had seen enough heartache and tragedy to last for a lifetime. On his first and subsequent liberties in Norfolk, Raymond did not, as Papa Miles would say, go out "seeking strange flesh."

After four months at Unit B-East, Raymond received his orders to go to sea. Life on an oil tanker was difficult. Old "salts" were accustomed to the run from Galveston to New York, to Iceland and to other ports. New boots who reported aboard the ship were given the worst assignments and were harassed by the older sailors. The term "cuss like a sailor" really had meaning on the ship, and one learned to curse as a method of survival. Cursing or bantering often rhymed, perhaps for emphasis.

During the wake-up call the head steward would come to the black quarters and blow a loud shrill sound on his whistle and invariably announce: "Reveille, Reveille, wake up and pee. See where your right hand caused your black ass to be." Amid laughter he would then announce, "Steward Greely didn't ask you to sign up. You signed on the dotted line. So I want every swinging dick to hit the deck now." His method

164

was effective and always the mess attendants responded with haste.

In early June of 1941, Raymond was assigned to the U.S.S. *Salinas*, an oil tanker that made frequent runs from Galveston, Texas to New York City and sometimes to Reykjavik, Iceland. So Raymond's first post as a seagoing sailor was Galveston. Along with his more experienced shipmates he was given a 48-hour pass for liberty in that city. After hitting a couple of clubs on Saturday night, they spent most of Sunday on the "colored only" beach where they met and shared a wholesome afternoon and evening with several girls from Houston-Tillotson College in Austin. Galveston was a relatively large city, but also a quiet city. It was nothing like Norfolk with its wicked and trashy Church Street. To Raymond, it was another Natchez, but just more of it. And the cultured young women reminded him of those at Sweethill College. It was a city that he wanted to visit again, but as fate would have it, that was his first and last trip to Galveston.

Within the next fifteen days his ship would be at Staten Island in New York City. The old salts on his ship had assured him that the Big Apple was no Galveston. They promised to give him the wildest and most exciting liberty—one that he would never forget. As the *Salinas* approached the New York Harbor, Raymond was amazed at the tall skyline. He had read so much about New York, but he had never dreamed that one day he would go there. He had heard the Hit Parade featuring the latest songs on his battery-powered radio in the country. He had heard big bands coming from the Apollo Theatre or other points in New York. He had heard about Broadway and had once seen a traveling version of Shakespeare's *Othello*. But being in New York and seeing it with his own eyes was over-whelming.

Late Friday evening, Raymond and his fellow shipmates began 48 hours of liberty in the largest city in the United States. They took the Staten Island ferry to Manhattan and viewed with amazement the Statue of Liberty in the harbor, then caught an uptown subway to 125th Street in Harlem. They took a room at the beautiful and well-known Hotel Theresa. With his shipmates he set out on a two-day spree which would forever live in his memory. When sailors enter a city, they do not generally seek out the cultural or historic spots for which the city is noted. Rather, they look for excitement which expresses itself in wine, women and song. In New York they found this in superabundance. The fact that Raymond's salary had been raised from $21 to $30 per month meant that he had a few extra dollars to spend.

After a dinner of hot dogs, hamburgers and beer from one of the small eateries, they headed to the famous Apollo Theatre to hear Woodie Herman and his Thundering Herd play among other tunes "Wood Choppers Ball." The show also featured the comedian Pigmeat Markham, who told racial jokes about both black and white folks. At that time, large numbers of whites went "slumming" in Harlem, so the theatre had as many whites as blacks in the audience that evening. In addition to enjoying the syncopating music of Woodie Herman, Raymond was elated over the fact that he was free to rub shoulders with white men and women without thinking about getting lynched. As he saw mixed couples sitting and embracing or walking arm in arm, he wondered, "How can black men be so free in one section of the country and virtually enslaved in another?" What he didn't realize was that this freedom was only a veneer, because economically and socially African-Americans were gradually being confined in a black ghetto which would become more restrictive as the years went by.

166

The leave took them to such clubs as the Baby Grand, the Cotton Club, Muranio's, and Small's Paradise, and ended at the world-renowned Savoy Ballroom. The Savoy was featuring Cooti Williams' Band with young Pearl Bailey as the soloist. As Raymond walked upstairs, he was conscious of his last dance-hall experience—the Rhythm Club in Natchez. He looked around for the exits and noticed that there were several and that the windows were not barred. Nevertheless, an eerie feeling came over him as he entered. With a conscious effort, his developing dance-hall phobia was pushed to the back of his mind so he could enjoy the excitement of this new place.

When the music became fast and hot, dancers jumped onto the floor and began expressing themselves uninhibitedly. As individual couples wildly moved their feet and bodies, popped their fingers and clapped their hands, a circle would form around them and mass clapping and yelling would begin. With urging from the crowd, the dancers gave full expression to the Lindy Hop, Jitterbug, Susie Q, Big Apple, or other dances. One could see from these dances, with each individual trying to create new steps, why so many good dances were born in Harlem.

Raymond knew that he was not going to dance in the Savoy Ballroom because his memories of Natchez, the Rhythm Club and Jean were too painful and vivid. However, several of his shipmates were pulled onto the floor by the "Savoy regulars" and they gave themselves body and soul to the dance. One sailor was jitterbugging and enjoying himself with a "girl" named "Rog" until somebody yelled out that Rog was a fairy. The sailor left the dance circle immediately amid laughter with an embarrassed look and sheepish grin on his face. Being one of Steward Ferguson's boys from Unit B-East he had learned to "hate a sissy like he hates a skunk." Yet he had been deceived into dancing with one! To show his masculinity, after the music stopped the sailor ran over to Rog and said: "You cock-sucking fairy, I got a good mind to kick your punking ass." As his shipmates pulled the sailor away, Rog stood with hands over blushing lips, showing absolutely no fear whatsoever.

As the sailors left the Savoy, Moon, the leader of the pack, said: "On liberty a good sailor should get boozed, screwed and tattooed. I'm all boozed up, so follow me, boys and let's go get screwed." They walked across 141st Street to a large first-floor apartment and rang the doorbell. A stately madam came to the door and welcomed the seven sailors. They were ushered to a well-appointed living room and each was offered the standard 50-cent shot of liquor. When Raymond, who was a teetotaler, refused the drink, the madam wanted to know what kind of sailor was this who didn't drink. "Is there anything else that he can't do?" she asked. Everybody laughed.

Shortly afterward, four scantily clad girls—three black and one white—came into the room and a quiet, demure-looking brown-skinned girl called Peaches walked over and sat on the side of Raymond's chair. She talked with Raymond for a couple of minutes and was amused when he told her that he was from Mississippi. A minute or so later, Raymond was following Peaches into a back room after paying his $2.50 to the call house madam. Raymond could not imagine why he had accepted Peaches' invitation since he had never dealt with a whore and, frankly, he thought whores were sinful and repulsive. Perhaps it was his desire to show his fellow shipmates that he was macho, to gain acceptance with the group since he didn't drink.

168

In the room, Raymond was an emotional disaster. Peaches walked over to the bed, neatly pulled up her short dress and laid across the bed with her legs slightly drawn up and partly open. Raymond stood there slightly startled with only three of the 13 buttons on his pants unbuttoned.

"Hurry up, baby," she called.

When a minute passed and Raymond was making little or no progress, the impatient call girl said: "Come on, you Mississippi boy, and do whatever in the hell you're going to do. I'm a working girl and I ain't got all night."

Raymond started buttoning up the three buttons that he had opened. The disappointed whore got up, straightened her hair and neatly adjusted her short skirt. On her way out, she said, "What's wrong with you, baby? I know I'm a good woman, so it's nothing wrong with me." With a pat on his crotch, she continued, "Are you all man?" As the two walked back to the waiting room, Raymond's buddies laughed and said: "Here comes the Rabbit, the Rabbit." Somebody laughingly said: "Boy, she sho knocked your rocks off quick. You didn't stay in there as long as John stayed in the Army. He went in at one and came out at one."

Raymond laughed with them but he was dying inside, not because he hadn't gone to bed with Peaches and certainly not because the boys called him a rabbit. He was appalled at the ease with which he had forgotten his Christian upbringing and how easily he had been persuaded to yield to temptation. He had been in New York City for less than a day and he allowed himself to be led by a group of sailors whose only goal in life was to become "boozed, screwed and tattooed." He wondered whether he would ever have the courage to stand alone for the values he had been taught. Would he be forever be "seeking strange flesh" trying to be acceptable to others? Sitting dejectedly in the corner of the waiting room, Raymond grew up. He pledged to himself that he would never allow himself to be caught in another whorehouse again. Deep down in his soul, he agreed with Papa Miles that such action was sin and "the wages of sin is death."

The 48-hour leave in New York City was, indeed, unforgettable. Raymond had seen the glamour places in Harlem and had been an unwilling participant in a brothel. While he found life in the Big Apple exciting, the rowdy and carefree life of the sailor was one that he could never internalize. Somehow, he thought, there has to be more to life than the epicurean excesses of eating, drinking, and making merry.

After a long and rough trip to Iceland, the U.S.S. *Salinas* returned to Norfolk, its home port. There Raymond was hospitalized with acute appendicitis and underwent immediate surgery. His ship returned to Galveston without him, and he was never to serve on that ship again.

During his recuperation period, Raymond visited the black USO in Norfolk where he would meet and socialize with girls from the Banks Street Junior College. The activities were fairly well supervised and chaperoned, much as they were at Sweethill College. After a few days, he developed a keen interest in Madge Norman, the daughter of the principal of a small-town school in the Chesapeake Bay area, who was attending Banks Street Junior college. After a week together, their relationship was becoming closer and more intimate. One night as they returned to Madge's dormitory, she began to cry and soon became hysterical. Patiently, Raymond consoled her as they sat quietly on a bench outside her dormitory. There she confided in Raymond her problems that had virtually brought her to the point of suicide. She was almost convinced that death was more desirable than going back home and facing the hostility, ostracism and social abuse that a small Christian community can mete out to its own children.

Madge had left her small rural town of nine hundred to study at the junior college with the idea of returning home and becoming a teacher. She was advised by her father and mother, a principal and teacher, respectively, to avoid sailors like the plague. She had assured them that she could handle herself in Norfolk, and that she would never seriously look at a sailor. In her mind she truly believed that sailors were low-life trash that a decent, God-fearing girl should not be caught dead with.

That was until the Saturday evening that she walked in the USO and met a handsome, smooth, fast-talking sailor named Taylor Barrow from Charleston, South Carolina. In the course of the evening, she told him of the promise that she had made to her parents to avoid sailors like the plague. He laughingly responded, "Don't listen to your parents, baby—I can tell you more about life in fifteen minutes than they told you in fifteen years." Madge knew that she should have stopped right then, but somehow she had to show him that his teachings were not stronger than her parents'.

Before her midnight curfew at the dormitory, Taylor had taken her to a tavern for a couple of drinks. Since she had never had as many as two drinks before, she was putty in his hands. Arm in arm they walked directly to Taylor's rented room. When Madge hesitated and suggested that maybe she shouldn't go in, Taylor picked up and carried a slightly kicking Madge over the threshold. Inside, Madge surrendered herself completely to Taylor. In their moments of ecstasy, she forgot all the prohibitions and defenses that her parents had taught her for more than fifteen years. To her, it was a first night of love; to Taylor, it was merely another night on the town.

It was only after her return to the dormitory just before curfew that she fully recognized her tragic mistake and the possible impact that the night could have on her life. She realized that she knew absolutely nothing about Taylor—not even the ship to which he was assigned. When he didn't call the next morning as he had promised, Madge went to the rooming house where he had taken her. Unfortunately the sailor knew she as Taylor Barrow had gone, and the landlord at the rooming house merely knew him as "a sailor who rents a room here sometimes." Madge walked back to her dormitory in a daze and with a heavy heart. In her soul, she knew that she had disobeyed her parents' teaching, and, in doing so, had played the fool with someone she didn't even know. She was never to hear from Taylor again.

Madge learned that she was pregnant the next month. The doctor told her he would perform an abortion for $50.00 if she could find some way to stay out of the dormitory for the weekend. But Madge did not have the fifty dollars, and she had some personal conflicts that had to be resolved.

Madge had been reared in a fundamentalist Christian home. She knew that fornication was a sin and the Bible condemned fornicators to hell. She had always maintained that she would be a virgin when she married. She knew that she had violated her parents' teachings and was now in a position to bring total disgrace upon the people whom she loved most. She believed that an abortion would constitute a deliberate killing of her own flesh and blood. Did not the Ten Commandments say

172

"Thou shalt not kill"? Rather than return to her small community and bring shame upon her parents and herself, she seriously considered suicide. But she viewed suicide as an unpardonable sin, and could not stand the thought that her soul would spend eternity in hell.

Raymond was visibly shaken by Madge's account of her problems and the social, emotional and spiritual conflicts which made it so difficult for her to deal with them. His experiences at Sweethill College and his ordeal in Natchez enabled him to understand the depth to which her spirit had fallen. Thus, he empathized with her so completely that he said, without weighing the consequences, "Don't you worry Madge, and just throw that word `suicide' out of your vocabulary. I'll help you. I'll be with you every step of the way. You're too nice a girl and came from too good a family to let one slick-ass sailor destroy your beautiful life."

For awhile they sat quietly with Raymond's arm around Madge and her head on his shoulder. He reflected on his own plight at Sweethill College a little more than one year before. He knew firsthand how devastating it can be to the human spirit when suddenly all dreams are shattered; when a generation gap renders loving parents useless; when previously held concepts of social justice and ethical living no longer square with reality; and when religious teachings, which are supposed to undergird all aspects of life, are of little or no significance for practical social adjustments. Raymond knew that this was not a time to debate the right and wrong of what had befallen Madge. It was a time for practical solutions that would enable her to get on with her life. He remembered how Ida, the student nurse at Sweethill, had consoled him and had helped to give him the will to live. He remembered how completely he had put his life in Dr. Sims' hands, a man who knew everything and had been everywhere. He remembered how Evella, his schoolmate, had forced him to face the public by walking all over town in spite of his physical appearance or emotions. So it was now his turn to be a shoulder that Madge could truly lean on. Somehow he had to convince this desperate girl to trust the goodwill of another sailor whom she did not know, and also to rely on a loving and forgiving God rather than a God of wrath.

Finally, Raymond spoke. "It'll be at least two weeks before I will be assigned to another ship, and if you let me, I will help you." With those words he could feel Madge's tense body relax, and suddenly she began to sob openly.

Between sobs, she kissed his cheeks and snuggled closer to Raymond and finally said: "I knew you were my guardian angel."

Raymond spoke firmly to her. "My way of helping is a rational, non-emotional, irreligious method. Regardless of what your religion or your God tells you, you must get an abortion and get it now. I have about $100 in cash back at the base. I'll pay the doctor $50 and I can put you up in a room for the weekend, and you can go back to school on Monday."

"But Raymond, I can't kill my own baby. I just can't."

"Don't be foolish, Madge," Raymond said. "It's really not a baby yet. You can rightfully have an abortion if the purpose is to save the mother's life. Back at Sweethill College, old Dr. Sims used to say that there are two types of abortion—criminal and therapeutic. If there is a medical or health reason, if it is in response to rape or incest, it is therapeutic. Since you were overpowered and virtually raped by a damned no-good sailor, an abortion can be socially, morally and religiously justified. Okay?"

"It sounds okay," said Madge, "but I'm so scared. I'm scared to death."

"You might be scared to do it," Raymond said, "but take it from someone who knows, it's a damn sight better than going back to your Chesapeake Bay town—to the wagging tongues and hostile stares of the hypocritical townfolks. Also, it's a damn sight better than suicide, that nonsense that you were talking about when I met you. So just convince yourself that this is a therapeutic abortion designed to save the mother's life. On Friday evening, we will be in the doctor's office and do what we must do to save your life. You'll confirm the appointment and I'll get the room at a rooming house, and we'll pray that everything will go smoothly and with little or no pain for you."

Madge agreed and seemed quite relieved. "But I can't do anything to repay you. I would never be able to get that much money from my parents, and I'm not physically or emotionally capable of giving my love to anyone anymore, so . . . "

Raymond stopped her abruptly. "You don't owe me anything, and certainly you don't owe me romantic love. Just let me be your guardian angel who came along at the right time. My reward will be getting you well and seeing you return to school and become a good teacher. Now I had better get back to the naval base." He kissed her softly on the cheek, but Madge kissed him firmly on his lips as she placed both arms around his shoulders. "Thank you, my guardian angel," she said.

Raymond replied, "I'll see you on Friday evening shortly after four o'clock."

On Friday afternoon, Raymond rented a room for the weekend for $2.50 in the same rooming house to which Taylor Barrow had taken Madge nearly two months ago. While he understood the trauma that Madge would experience in going back there again, Raymond knew that the anonymity she desired would be protected there. Madge had arranged a trip home with one of her roommates, and had her parents' approval to stay out of the dorm for the weekend.

The doctor performed what he called "a smooth and non-threatening operation," gave her antibiotics and pain pills, and advised her to stay off her feet for three days. Once Madge had made up her mind to begin the process, she turned out to be a real trooper. Raymond got a cab and took her to the rooming house. The cab driver said to Raymond as he drove away, "Don't have too much fun tonight, sailor." Little did the driver know that it was not fun that he was seeking. Rather, he was seeking an answer to his prayer that Madge would heal satisfactorily and would be able to return to class and school activities without detection or difficulties.

Raymond took Madge back to the dormitory on Sunday evening and watched her walk gingerly up the one flight of stairs toward her room. She went to classes on Tuesday, and on Saturday she told Raymond by telephone that "she was out of the woods" and was on her way to full recovery in her physical health and in her classroom work. In the meantime, Raymond received his new orders to report to the U.S.S. *Palmer*, a converted destroyer/minesweeper, at the Norfolk Naval Base. They said their goodbyes on the phone. She promised to write often. As Raymond packed his duffle bag in readiness for his new assignment, he thought, "During a time of severe personal crisis all you really need is a true and firm shoulder to lean on—someone to be a `good Samaritan' and

176

help restore you to honor, dignity and wholeness." In this case, Raymond had been that good Samaritan, and he felt happy that he had been in a position to help.

Raymond's new orders required him to report to Pier 7 at the Norfolk Naval Base on Sunday evening for duty on the U.S.S. *Palmer*. Raymond was placed in the all-black messman quarters, and was assigned to the officers' dining hall on Sunday evening. But early during the week, he made a terrible mistake. He saw a sign on the bulletin board which said: "Any sailor who has any typing skills should check with the Yeoman First Class about training for the position." Since Raymond could type about 40 words per minute, he honestly saw this as a way out of the Messmen's Branch. When he applied and told the Yeoman First Class his abilities, the yeoman said, "I don't care how fast you can type, we don't use Negras in this branch." Raymond's spirit was crushed. He walked out of his quarters determined that the Navy was not the place for him—that somehow, he had to get out of the Navy.

Without consulting anyone, he wrote a letter to the Bureau of Navigation, which then controlled the Navy, asking for permission to transfer from the Navy to the Army. To his surprise, the Bureau sent the letter to the commanding officer of the ship. Since it was a court martial offense to write the Bureau without going through protocol, Raymond was found guilty of violating naval protocol and sentenced to three days of bread and water in the brig. After spending a few hours in the brig, he was taken to Captain C.C. Milner's quarters, the Commander of all minesweepers in the area. Captain Milner gave him a very stern, fatherly lecture which reminded Raymond of Papa Miles. He told Raymond that he had done wrong in writing the Bureau, but that he could understand how a boy with college training must feel by being restricted to the Messmen's Branch. He told him that he could do absolutely nothing about that. However, he advised: "For the duration of your time, just learn to be the best damn mess attendant in the Navy. Save your money, invest some of your money, and when you get out, go to Tuskegee Institute and get you a degree in agriculture. Then, like Booker T. Washington, you can become a leader of your people. Do you understand me, boy?"

Raymond answered, "Aye, aye, Sir."

Captain Milner continued: "I will clear your record and will send you to the next class at the Cooks' and Bakers' School for messmen in San Diego, California. If you can complete that course in the top quarter of your class, you should be able to earn your rate of first class steward quickly. With your training and intelligence, you should be a good admiral's steward. In the meantime, I am going to let you work with Steward Mendosa, in my quarters." He then called Steward Mendosa and introduced him to Raymond, and told him that Raymond would be working with him. Mendosa, who was a Filipino, told Raymond outside the door that Negroes did not make good Captain's and Admiral's stewards, so he was taking him only because he had to.

Three weeks later, Raymond was in a segregated coach of a Jim Crow train en route to a week's leave in Mississippi and then on to California to begin the next class at the Cooks' and Bakers' School.

Captain Milner had arranged Pullman car accommodations for Raymond. This enabled him to sleep at nights in the end bunk of the sleeping coach and eat in the segregated section of the dining coach during the days. So when the train pulled into Corapeake, his relatives, friends, and curious onlookers were waiting for black people to disembark from the black section. When Mama and Papa Miles were about to conclude that Raymond was not on the train, they saw him walking with his bag from the white section. After greeting him, the first thing that Papa Miles said was, "Son, Corapeake is the same today as it was yesterday. So stay in your place and don't rock the boat. White people still beat and lynch niggers in this town who don't know their places." Raymond knew that when Papa Miles had made up his mind it was useless to say anything to try to change it. So he just listened the same way he used to do when he was a little boy. He did not try to tell him that he was merely following naval orders and was not fighting racial policies in Corapeake.

After several quiet and peaceful days in the countryside near Corapeake with his family, Raymond reluctantly visited Natchez. This was his first time in Natchez since the fire on April 23, 1940 which killed 209 black citizens, including his fiancee, Jean Gravier. Once in Natchez, he went first to the charred Rhythm Club which was still standing. Although it was boarded up, he pushed his body through a small opening and walked around in the club that had been the scene of so much sorrow and grief. Next he went to the National Undertaking Company. The undertaker permitted Raymond to look through 59 burial certificates and observe the methods that were used to try to identify 39 unidentified bodies. Since National handled Jean Gravier's body for burial, and since she was interred in the family burial plot, it was not difficult to find her gravesite. He purchased two roses, drove to the grave, and placed the roses with stems crossed upon her tomb. As he said a silent prayer, he was touched by the shortness of her life—January 10, 1923 to April 23, 1940. What a tragedy, he thought, for God to take such a beautiful and charming young lady who had just begun to live.

About mid-afternoon, Raymond visited the Gravier home and was warmly received. Almost immediately, Mrs. Gravier served ice cream and cake. While she knew that Raymond was eager to talk about Jean, she very skillfully avoided the subject by asking Raymond about various phases of life in the Navy. When Raymond finished his ice cream and cake he spoke up: "Mr. and Mrs. Gravier, I got to say this. I feel so hurt and so guilty that I must tell you how sorry I am that I caused Jean's death."

Mrs. Gravier broke in immediately. "Just hush that kind of talk, my dear boy. You didn't cause Jean's death any more than I did. You did all that you could do to save her. So it's nobody's fault. It was God's will. When we pray and say `Thy will be done,' we had better mean it. For God moves in a mysterious way. So stop blaming yourself as we did a long time ago. Because `the Lord giveth and the Lord taketh away, Blessed be the name of the Lord.' Join me," she told Raymond, "in saying, `Blessed be the name of the Lord.'" She then gave Raymond the picture of Jean that he had requested. In her kind motherly way, she advised him, "Raymond, you are a good boy with fine home training. Jean is dead and she isn't going to come back. You may cherish her memory as I do, but there are many fine girls out there waiting for a fine young man like you. You'll find the one for you. Just remember that, and always come back to see us when you are in Natchez." Raymond bade the Graviers farewell and prepared to return to Corapeake.

On his way out of Natchez, Raymond made two quick stops. The first was the Bluff Park Monument, a relatively small upright stone structure overlooking the Mississippi River and bearing the names of the 209 persons who died as a result of the Natchez fire. A memorial service had been held at the monument on the first anniversary of the fire by the interracial ministerial alliance of Natchez. As Raymond pulled away, he wondered what impact the people in Natchez would have if they had cooperated in life as they did in death.

Near the outskirts of Natchez, Raymond stopped in a little juke-joint to buy a soda pop. Although Mississippi was a dry state, no sooner had he walked in than a teenage waitress asked him if he would like to buy a half-pint of bourbon. Raymond refused and purchased his soft drink. Shortly, the piccolo blasted out with a blues number that Raymond had never heard before called "Natchez Burning" or "The Burning in that Natchez, Mississippi Town." The short and poorly composed lyrics described the burning at the Rhythm Club, named the people who were there, summarized the fire's devastating effects, and ended with a rhythmic and emotional moaning characteristic of chattel slaves on the plantation. People were dancing and having a good time to music about 209 black fellow citizens who had experienced a tragic death in that city. Raymond was upset. "How can black people make merry while listening to a song about the death of 209 of their people—people who died in a black holocaust—a firetrap that was a monument to racial segregation and to social injustice for black people?" A tragic event had become a source of entertainment for black people who were apparently unaware that the sordid tentacles of oppression and segregation had so completely captured them, body and soul. Society had completely robbed them of the capacity to even think about human dignity, much less fight for it.

Raymond remembered the winding and rough canopy-covered Natchez Trace, the road his family had taken when they brought him home from the hospital at Sweethill College. On that occasion he had been tense and scared; this time he was relieved and pensive. Somehow he was beginning to internalize, as Mrs. Gravier had instructed him, that in good and in evil, in good times and in sorrow, we must be ready to let the Lord's will be done. This trip back home was thought-provoking and cleansing. He could now see clearly that humankind does not control its own destiny. More and more he was beginning to recognize that seeing problems as the Lord's will is excellent emotional therapy.

On the last night of vacation in Corapeake, Raymond and his family went to their country church for the annual box supper. Ladies would prepare a box of food and men would bid on the box and be given the option of eating with the lady who prepared the box. Raymond purchased a box for the relatively large sum of $2.50 which was prepared by his classmate, Evella. He was not so much concerned about the quality of the meal in Evella's box as he was about the opportunity to talk with her. He would always be grateful to her for helping him to face the public last year after his burns in the Natchez fire, and he wanted to tell her so. In his short conversation with Evella, he learned that she had married an uneducated farm boy, and lived in the country about seven miles west of Corapeake. Already she had two small children and was beginning to look plain and unkempt. It was a tense dinner because Raymond could feel the jealous eyes of Evella's husband on him all the time. Also, he could see how uncomfortable Evella was as they tried to talk. So he hurriedly finished his dinner and walked around and talked with other church members, even the members of the church council that had planned to expel him from the church.

Upon leaving the church, Raymond reflected on the plight of Evella. She had been class valedictorian, and was voted the girl most likely to succeed. But because her family was large and poor, she could not find the support to go to Sweethill College. So she did what black Mississippi girls were expected to do at that time—marry farm boys or sawmill hands and produce others like them to be exploited by the white race. Although he enjoyed the food and the fellowship of the evening, his heart was heavy. Here was a highly intelligent woman with so much promise who, because of her color, was destined to live out her life as a victim of racial oppression, and to waste her talents in the closed, segregated society of Mississippi.

The next morning, Raymond said his farewell to his family amid kisses, hugs and tears. Once more he boarded the Bee heading for New Orleans, this time to make connections with the Sunset Limited train to San Diego, California. Again, he went to the home of his Uncle Ozzie and Aunt Lizzie in New Orleans and ate some of the best gumbo in the world. Despite the good food, the four-hour layover in New Orleans could not pass fast enough. The whole conversation centered around the likelihood of war, and the evils of Raymond's participation in that war. Already, Hitler had released his fury in Europe, overrun Poland and Czechoslovakia, and was threatening to dominate France and Great Britain. It appeared likely that the United States would be drawn into the war. Thus, Raymond would have to fight in an unholy, evil war—a war solely for the purpose of maintaining the white man's way of life. As they drove Raymond back to the Union Station, Aunt Lizzie gave him this admonition: "Find a way to get out of that Navy, because nothing good will come to a man who fights in a war to preserve evil."

As the train pulled out of New Orleans en route to San Diego, Raymond recalled that when he left for Norfolk nine months earlier, Aunt Lizzie had warned him that "nothing good would happen to him." New Orleans was a city noted for voodooism and fortunetelling, and Raymond could not push Aunt Lizzie's warning from his consciousness as the train headed west and faded into the sunset.

Chapter XII

E very black boy or girl in Mississippi longed to escape the clutches of racial segregation by going to Chicago or California. While Chicago was the most accessible land of freedom, California—from San Diego to Los Angeles to San Francisco—was viewed as a veritable paradise. At Corapeake High School, Raymond would occasionally sing on stage or participate in school plays. As crude as his performances were, somehow he honestly thought that if he could get to Hollywood, he could one day become a movie star. Of course, this was a dream that was unlikely to come true. However, the beauty of dreams is that they do not require realistic foundations. They provide the elasticity by which the horizon of even the most oppressed souls can be expanded; but they may also fuel depression that may plunge the emotionally weak into the darkest abyss. Raymond had at one time or another found himself at both ends of the dream spectrum.

But on this Thursday morning, he was in California, just a few miles away from San Diego. He was not in California seeking his fame in the movie capital of the world as he once dreamed. Rather, he was on a realistic journey to six weeks of preparation in the Navy's Cooks' and Bakers' School to make him more proficient at serving white officers. He recognized that California would not automatically bring liberation and freedom to him, but would merely make him a better servant— a better "hewer of wood and drawer of water."

Fifty black sailors began the course with him and forty-eight completed it six weeks later. They had an integrated, dedicated staff of instructors who were determined to make them the elite messmen stewards and cooks in the Navy, since fewer than five percent of black sailors were afforded this special training. In addition to the art of cooking and baking, they were taught manners, appropriate decorum and etiquette of serving in officers' messes, especially high-ranking officers. Raymond knew that when he finished the course, he would be hooked for the duration in the Messmen's Branch, so he concentrated on perfecting his skills in baking.

After the second weekend, the sailors were given weekend liberty in San Diego. Although blacks could go to most theaters, eat at some restaurants, and use all public parks and facilities, as in most other cities, their social life was virtually restricted to black establishments. Except for a few places on Imperial Avenue, blacks congregated at the Creole Palace and the Douglass Hotel. The Creole Palace provided the booze and contact point for the girls, and the Douglass Hotel provided the sleeping quarters.

Raymond's first forty-eight-hour pass in San Diego was enjoyable and eventful. As he walked into the Creole Palace, he noticed a young girl and an older woman sitting at a table eating their lunch. His eyes met the warm response of the younger girl, and almost instinctively he started walking toward their table. The older woman said: "Why don't you join us here and have some lunch? They serve fine lunches here."

Raymond, a little shocked, said: "I think I will get a drink, but I've already had my lunch."

He sat down and introduced himself, told them amid laughs that he was from Mississippi, and that he was in San Diego for a six-week training course in Cooks' and Bakers' School. The two ladies were from Longview, Texas and had been in San Diego for seven months. The younger girl, Dee Dee Moore, was a senior in high school. Almost as if it had been planned, the older woman, her cousin, she said, had to keep an appointment. "Take care of Dee Dee," she said as she rose to leave. "She's a good girl. I'm leaving her with you because I believe you are a good boy."

Raymond assured her that he was. At Dee Dee's suggestion, they went first to the world famous zoo in Balboa Park, to Old Town, and back to the Spreckles Theatre for a movie. The day was wonderful. Dee Dee was an olive-skinned girl who obviously wanted the best things in life and who loved and respected herself. Raymond could tell that she enjoyed showing him around. She had a special knack of listening attentively to Raymond's frustrations about segregation and limitations in the Navy. They were on the same wavelength and both said they believed in love at first sight. Raymond learned that Dee Dee was living on Imperial Avenue with her cousin, who was single, and since her conservative parents were not in California, she did not have a curfew. She could stay out as long as she wished. All her cousin expected her to do was to be careful.

After the movie, Raymond and Dee Dee stopped by the Creole Palace for a drink and dancing. Since Dee Dee didn't

187

drink and Raymond didn't drink, they both laughed about the Shirley Temples they ordered—trying to look the part. When Raymond came into town on his 48-hour pass, he had stopped by the Douglass to get a room before they were all sold out. So after the drink, he invited Dee Dee to come up to his room. Without hesitation she agreed.

As they walked toward the hotel lobby, Dee Dee paused for a minute and said, "I've got to ask you something that I hate to ask, and I hope you won't take it the wrong way. I've got to have ten dollars. Will you let me have it?"

In Raymond's mind, Dee Dee immediately became a hooker. He remembered the girl at the Astoria Hotel in New Orleans propositioning him for money; he remembered the hooker in New York who had beat him out of $2.50. And now after he had shown Dee Dee such a good time, she was trying to hit him for the unheard-of price of ten dollars. Raymond said cautiously, "What are you talking about? Ain't no woman in the world worth ten dollars."

Dee Dee appeared shocked. She placed both hands over her face and began to cry. Raymond tried to catch her arm, but she pulled it away; nevertheless she proceeded up two flights into Raymond's room. She sat down on the side of the bed, visibly shaken. Raymond moved over beside her and tried to place his arm around her waist. Then Dee Dee spoke up angrily.

"I do not sell my body, but I would give it to the man I love. I wanted the ten dollars to send my mother and father a gift on their twenty-fifth anniversary. I work part-time every day to make my own living, but I was a little short this week. I felt that I knew you so well that I could share anything with you. So when I told you that I needed ten dollars, you, like your other no-good sailor friends made me a prostitute—a low-down prostitute selling her body to any man."

Raymond begged, "Please forgive me, Dee Dee. When you've been around the Navy long enough, it's hard not to think that all women are out to take you. I understand now and I'm sorry as I can be. I'll be happy to let you have the ten dollars."

They sat together there on the side of the bed. Then Dee Dee spoke up again. "When your cold words—'ain't no woman worth ten dollars'—hit my ears, my first thought was to mess you up real bad. You see, I'm just sixteen years old and you are a man. I had planned to come up to your room and then cry rape. I'm what they call a 'San Quentin Quail' in California. So buddy, I thought about accusing you of statutory rape. But then I thought, how could you love a man almost at first sight and then destroy him. I couldn't. I just couldn't."

"Would you really have done that?" Raymond asked. Dee Dee replied: "I don't think I could have gone through with it, but I sure thought about it."

After this exchange, Dee Dee seemed to warm up a bit. Raymond took out the ten dollars and pleaded with her to take it. When he thought she was responding well to his embraces, he begged her to take off her clothes and stay with him awhile. But she refused. "I still need the ten dollars, and in spite of all that's been said, I'll take it. But it's no way that I could go to bed with you tonight. You've hurt me too much. So take my phone number and call me next week. If you want to see me then, I'll be home—not hustling on the streets."

Raymond kissed her passionately and watched as she walked out the door. A moment later, he caught her at the bus stop in time to say another good-bye.

Throughout the next month in San Diego, Raymond saw Dee Dee on all of his liberties and their love for each other made them feel that they could spend the rest of their lives together. But as with most sailors, the period of training ended quickly, and Raymond found new duty and a new girl in another port, and he and Dee Dee gradually drifted apart.

Upon completing his training at Cooks' and Bakers' School in San Diego, Raymond was given an award as the honor man in the class of 48 sailors. His skills in the baking and decoration of cakes, pies, and pastry placed him at the top of his class. The Naval commander in charge of the school praised Raymond for his accomplishments and assured him that he "had all of the tools and skills to become a top steward in an admiral's mess." He continued, "If your attitude is right, and if your work habits are good, you can get to the top in this man's Navy." He then invited Raymond to come forward for the cherished certificate.

As Raymond moved toward the commander to receive the certificate, he realized that the only times that he had ever been at the top of his class had occurred in the Navy. He was the honor man of Class 5 at Unit B-East in Norfolk, and now he was the honor man of Cooks' and Bakers' School in San Diego. In spite of himself, in spite of his disdain for the tasks to which he was assigned, Raymond could still be the best among his peers. Yet these honors had not encouraged him to try to be the best steward in the Navy, but had created a restiveness in him to seek a better status in life for himself.

Armed with his honor certificate, Raymond was sent to the man-made Treasure Island between San Francisco and Oakland to await assignment to the Pacific fleet. During the three-week wait, Raymond would occasionally take liberty in the

Fillmore and Geary Streets section of San Francisco, a section which was very much like Norfolk's Church Street. It was the black section of town and in it were many seedy joints, taverns, pimps, prostitutes and flophouses. It was not unusual to find apartment houses where single rooms had been cut in two with makeshift partitions for rental purposes. Housing was scarce for blacks and many people from the South were crowding into the black section weekly seeking the good life. Many started in these meager circumstances and were soon able to move on to better things. But far too many became the victims of fast living and exploitation by city slickers. The social headquarters for sailors in San Francisco was the Flamingo Club, located in the heart of the Fillmore district. Here one could find everything from "reefers to razors."

On one of Raymond's shore liberties, as he was entering the Flamingo, he was amazed to meet Sally Mae Cousins, a schoolmate from Corapeake, who had escaped the shackles of oppression there and found her way to California—the western promised land. He embraced Sally Mae, sat at the table reminiscing about the simple and restrictive life that they had lived back home, and about the joys and sorrows of school life at Corapeake High. Raymond invited her to share a full evening of dinner and entertainment with him.

"I don't think I can, Raymond. I've got something planned. Maybe I can get out of it and meet you later," she said. "I really want to , I really do but, but . . ." Raymond wondered why Sally Mae appeared so nervous. He sensed that something was wrong. Then out of the corner of his eye he saw a well-dressed man in a zoot suit and a wide-brimmed hat standing just inside the door who was beckoning to Sally Mae. Raymond asked: "Is that dude by the door your boyfriend?"

"No. He's just a friend. He helped me a little when I first got here. But he's nothing to me."

She finished her drink hurriedly and was getting her purse when all of a sudden the well-dressed man walked over to the table, snatched her up and made a motion as if to strike her. So as to be sure that Raymond heard, he said: "Whenever I call you, bitch, I want you to bring your ass to me right then, understand? Understand?"

Sally said in a muted voice, "Yes."

He continued, "You can't waste your time in here screwing around with this nigger sailor." With a firm grip on her arm, he dragged her out the door. Raymond wanted to help Sally Mae, but he saw that she was nothing but a cheap prostitute and the man was her ass-whipping pimp. The pimp was not about to let Sally Mae lose an evening socializing with a square sailor like him when there were hundreds of other sailors out there with money to spend, who were looking for a lay. Raymond doubted whether Sally Mae really wanted to be helped.

Raymond walked to the door and he could see Sally Mae and her pimp in a heated argument—the man struck her and pushed her down the street. Raymond had been taught that any man worth the salt in his bread would protect the dignity of womanhood. Nevertheless, he could not bring himself to get involved. His experience of nine months in the Navy had convinced him that Sally Mae had already lost all of the honor and dignity that she had ever had. She was nothing but a whore whose life and being were determined by the whims of her pimp. If she didn't like her life, she had certainly learned to adjust to it.

He went back to the table and sat by himself for a few moments. He saw plainly that oppressors and even slaveholders

192

could be people of any color. Those who are motivated by greed can easily suppress the rights and freedoms of others to satisfy their own needs. Color of skin is not the major factor in the domination and exploitation of others. So Sally Mae, who had been sexually abused from the time she was an adolescent by the white man she worked for, had simply traded her white oppressor for a black oppressor. One could argue that the black one was worse than the white. While the white man in Corapeake exploited her purely for his sexual needs, her black pimp put her on the block to be used by many for his personal financial gain. Sally Mae had, indeed, reached what people back home thought was the promised land, but she was headed toward destruction.

On Sunday morning, Raymond slept late in his Geary Street hotel. Raymond was determined that he would not let the fast life of the Navy destroy all of the values learned at the feet of Papa and Mama Miles. So he dressed and rushed out looking for a church. It was quarter past eleven, so he was already late. As he walked a couple of blocks down Geary Street, he heard religious music coming from a storefront church. He walked in and sat in the back and listened to a two-hour service of fire-and-brimstone preaching with lively and spirited music. Near the end of the service, the minister called for those who had not lived free from sin during the week to raise their hands. Raymond realized that he had not committed any grievous sins, yet he was not certain that he had lived free from sin. So he raised his hand. Two sisters came and escorted him to the "moaners bench" where the minister personally prayed that God would deliver Raymond from sin. He called on God to "lengthen out the brittle threads of this sailor's sinful life, and bid his moments on earth a little while to roll on." He further petitioned God "to snatch this man's foot from a burning hell." Raymond could have understood a sermon or prayer like that after the burning of the Rhythm Club, but this week he had not violated his home training or values.

After church, the Reverend Dr. Joshua Wright asked him to wait for a moment because he wanted to talk with him. To Raymond's surprise, Dr. Wright did not want to talk about living free from sin, but about how Raymond spent his liberties in San Francisco. The minister invited him to have a sundae with him at the nearby ice-cream parlor and Raymond accepted. The minister began to explain that he had a big spacious home that he had bought from the Japanese and that Raymond was free to stay there whenever he came on liberty.

Before Raymond could reply to this generous offer, he felt Wright's hand slightly pressing his knee. He tried not to pay any attention and kept eating his sundae, but as the minister began to move his hand progressively up his leg, Raymond remembered Steward Ferguson's advice to "avoid a punk like you would a skunk." Ferguson further advised his boys never to panic, but to look the punk in the eyes and reply in a positive and forceful manner. "A punk is like a white man—he can't look a mad nigger in the eye." So Raymond picked up one of the dull knives off the table which had been set for lunch. Looking Wright dead in the face he said: "If you don't take your goddamn hand off of me, I'll cut it off."

Wright quickly moved his hand. "I didn't mean what you think I meant," he said. "You misunderstood me." By that time the preacher was standing. Without further exchange, he paid the waitress and disappeared from the ice-cream parlor. When Wright left, the waitress came over to the table and repeated the preacher's line about a free home-away-from-home.

She knew that he frequently brought young men in and sometimes left with them. "I was glad that you didn't fall for his line...a hypocrite up there preaching the gospel in the morning and trying to pick up boys in the evening. You know he'll go to hell, won't he?" Raymond agreed with her as he left the parlor.

After three weeks in the San Francisco Bay area, Raymond was assigned to the U.S.S. *Pennsylvania*. He knew that after routine maneuvers he would spend most of his time at Pearl Harbor in Honolulu, Hawaii. While Honolulu was choice duty for white sailors, it was in many ways hell for black sailors. Whether in the continental United States or in its provinces or territorial possessions, black sailors could never forget that they were black. Blacks had more freedom here than in Mississippi, to be sure, because they could attend some public places, purchase a meal and see a show with few restrictions, but shore leave for blacks and whites was virtually segregated. Life on the naval base was also segregated.

Black sailors knew about going to the Two Jacks Bar long before arriving in Honolulu. This was the social and entertainment center for blacks on the island. Here they could dance and socialize with the few black women who had migrated to the island and with the few natives who frequented Two Jacks. Call houses in the area dealt effectively with both their white and black clientele by adopting a separate-but-equal policy. Blacks could be serviced by the same call girls for two dollars and fifty cents, but blacks would enter by a separate door and wait in the black waiting room. Since blacks were perceived as being better endowed than their white counterparts, most girls added an extra fifty cents for their service. The length of time was measured in ten-minute intervals. Although

Raymond himself did not frequent call houses, and had not been in one since his disastrous experience in New York, he had heard his fellow sailors give descriptive details of the differences in anatomy and sexual behavior among white, Japanese, Chinese, Hawaiian, and black hookers. To most sailors, getting "boozed, screwed and tattooed" was the ideal way to spend shore liberty, and most believed that variety was the spice of life. So they would try two or three nationalities or races each night.

During the latter part of November, the U.S.S. *Pennsylvania*, a battleship, pulled into the dry dock at Pearl Harbor for routine repairs and was third in line behind two other battleships. In turn, sailors would take liberty in Honolulu and spend the time at Two Jacks and in other centers of riotous living in the city. However, on the morning of December 7, 1941, carefree attitudes disappeared when the Japanese made their assault on the fleet at Pearl harbor. The attack came about five minutes to eight in the morning and lasted for about one and one half hours. Raymond was among the more than three thousand American casualties. The battleship fleet was virtually wiped out or immobilized and numerous small vessels were damaged or destroyed. The aircraft carriers were saved because they were outside the harbor. This so-called "Black Sunday" or day of infamy led the United States Congress to declare war on Japan four days later.

When "General Quarters," the call for all men to go to their assigned battle stations, was sounded on the U.S.S. *Pennsylvania*, Raymond ran to his station. Black sailors were generally required to work in the magazine or in positions requiring the passage of ammunition to white gun crews. Raymond's job was to push the ammunition onto a hoist on a conveyor belt, which lifted the ammunition to the topside. Had Raymond and his friends stayed at the original battle station they would have surely died. But when the large gun to which they were sending ammunition malfunctioned, they were pulled off that job and sent to supply other guns. There they had the responsibility of taking boxes of three-inch shells, four to a box, to a gun on the quarter deck. They stacked rows and rows of shells near the doorway to be taken to an inner room.

Just as Raymond and a friend from Clarksdale, Mississippi were carrying shells through the doorway to the inner room, a Japanese bomb hit the shells in that room. Raymond's friend was killed on the spot, but Raymond was knocked back through the door ten or twelve feet across the ship. Raymond lay immobilized on the deck with first-and second-degree burns and with several pieces of schrapnel in his body, but he remained conscious. This was indeed 'deja vu.' His experience of the black holocaust in Natchez permeated his thoughts, and pain took possession of his body.

Raymond was rushed to the naval base hospital with his body burning all over. His eyes felt like two coals of fire. In spite of his pain, he realized that he was blind. What would it be like to be blind at such a young age? In the emergency room, they covered his body with a tannic acid solution just as the doctor had done in Natchez and as Dr. Sims had done at Sweethill College. While Raymond knew from experience that tannic acid would minimize the pain from burns, he also knew that it would leave his flesh hard and crusty. The doctor worked on his eyes for what seemed like an eternity, then placed a gauze bandage over them. "Will I be blind, Doc?" Raymond asked.

"No, I don't think so. We'll keep a bandage on for two or three days and then we'll know for sure. My experience tells me that you will be able to see as usual," the doctor said.

"Thank you, doctor. I've got to see. I'd rather be dead than be burned and blind," said Raymond.

"You just relax and think about getting better. You're going to get well if you do what I tell you. I've treated burns much worse than yours."

Although Raymond could not see him, he knew that he was a white doctor because blacks were not allowed to practice in the Navy. But he sounded just like Dr. Sims at the Sweethill College Hospital, who gave his patients confidence by telling them that he had treated and brought back to health patients in more serious condition than they. Raymond felt that he had a good doctor who was devoted to saving lives, whether black or white.

For a few days there was a somber, fearful mood throughout Honolulu, because most people expected the Japanese to return and perhaps invade the island. The hospitals were filled with casualties, but even in the face of war and destruction the Navy found the energy and resources to separate the races. Just as housing and clubs were racially segregated, hospital facilities likewise always clustered blacks in the same area. Black people were being forced to fight and die for a way of life that dehumanized and oppressed them, and for a freedom they could never share.

Lying blind and burned in a hospital, one has time for reflection between sleep and pain. So Raymond reflected on the Rhythm Club fire at Natchez which had taken the lives of 209 black people. Segregation had caused blacks to seek entertainment in a firetrap. The fire department knew this, the police knew it, the mayor knew it, and the Money Wasters' Club knew it, but because the people who used it were black, nobody really cared.

Even in the wake of misery and death, when the white leaders of Natchez allowed some racial barriers to be removed, they could not give black citizens real equality even for a day. White doctors and nurses gave their services, to be sure, but white wards at hospitals were never opened to take care of emergencies. White doctors maintained their separate racial policies, white funeral homes did not embalm black bodies, and even white graveyards remained lily white. Whites who were willing to treat black people like human beings were afraid of the ostracism or condemnation that they would receive for their humane gestures.

Here in a military hospital more than five thousand miles from Mississippi, Raymond was finding the same sort of inhumanity to man that he had left in his home state. In a sense, he had experienced a second black holocaust. He had risked his life at the most dangerous of jobs—carrying and hoisting ammunition from a magazine to supply the white gunners—and had been nearly killed in the process. Now he found himself in the black section of a segregated hospital where second-rate attention was likely to be given to him. He reflected on what Aunt Lizzie told him in New Orleans, that white men are concerned only with money, power, and the protection of white women from black men. She had admonished him, "Nothing good will ever come to you for fighting in a white man's war to protect his way of life." It seemed that Aunt Lizzie's prediction had come to pass.

The flash of ammunition exploding on the U.S.S. *Pennsylvania* and the fire raging before huge fans in the Rhythm Club had one thing in common. For Raymond, both represented angels of death which force people to look backward. During his blindness he saw in his mind the lovely face of Jean Gravier, whose life had been senselessly ended at an early age by this same death angel. He could hear the very calm and trusting voice of Mrs. Gravier telling him to overcome his guilt feelings and say, "Thy will be done." He remembered the white family who had treated his burns—against social conventions—and sent him on his way. He remembered Sweethill College Hospital and Dr. Sims, a man who could instill confidence, and Ida, a student nurse who knew the real meaning of love. He remembered his Christian family who in their own way gave love and understanding from their perspective in a home where he had brought so much shame and disappointment. He thought about Ceily, the Church Council, Evella and the impact that each had on his life. He considered J.C.'s lynching, Bulldog Johnson's control of black town, and the depraved and meaningless lives that so many blacks had learned to accept. Despite it all, he thought, "If I had my choice, I'd rather be in Mississippi with people who know me, than to bear my burdens here alone."

Raymond knew that his shipmate from Clarksdale, Mississippi had died in the blast, and he felt more alone than ever. The white hospital corpsman who checked on him would always say: "How you doing this morning, boy?", or in a more friendly mood, "How's my boy doing today?" The condescending remarks he made would pierce Raymond to his heart, but he simply sucked it up and said nothing. This experience convinced Raymond that there is nothing like being incapacitated in a strange land among strange people, especially if you are black. So when all else seemed to fail, Raymond would pray. As Mama Miles would say: "When you've done all that you can do, just take your burdens to the Lord and leave them there." As farfetched as it sounded, in the time of crisis, it was real food for the soul and even therapy for the body.

On the third day the bandages were removed from his eyes and the first thing Raymond saw was a smiling, gentle white doctor looking down on him. With real pleasure and satisfaction he told Raymond: "I knew you'd be able to see, and with a few skin grafts, no one would ever know you were burned. In your sleep and while you were delirious, you talked about home a lot. So in about twenty days or so, I'm going to recommend a short vacation at home."

Raymond thanked the doctor and briefly told him about his close call with death in Natchez. The doctor himself was a graduate of the University of Mississippi and knew all about the fire. Raymond told the doctor that he reminded him so much of Dr. Sims back at Sweethill College. The white doctor knew a great deal about Sweethill, but he didn't ask Raymond whether Dr. Sims was black or white.

During twenty days of recuperation and sharing with other black sailors, Raymond learned that practically all of the U.S.S. *Arizona*'s stewards and cooks were killed when that ship went down from a direct hit. They talked proudly about the unusual heroism of Dorie Miller, a black mess attendant on the U.S.S. *Arizona*. He was given credit for manning a machine gun that he had never been taught to operate, and successfully destroyed two of the attacking Japanese aircraft. The crippled and burned sailors at the hospital took pride in talking about the foolish use of black manpower. Most felt that they, like Dorie Miller, could have brought down several planes if only they had been given a chance. As one sailor summed it up: "In war, I don't want no cracker protecting me. Just gimme a gun and I'll protect myself."

As the doctor promised, Raymond was allowed a two-week vacation at home. Again Raymond was going home with his hands burned and white splotches on his face and body, but this time something was different. He was going home a hero. When he had come home from Sweethill College, he had carried the burden of having betrayed the trust of his parents by going to a dance hall. He had carried with him the guilt of being a participant in the death of a girl he loved. He had faced the shame of being kicked out of school, thus bringing disgrace on his upright Christian family. His immature outlook on life had made him unable to face up to the physical marks that the fire had left on him that time. And he had been filled with a yearning to get the hell out of Mississippi with its history of racial segregation and oppression. The Navy provided that avenue of escape.

This time he was returning home with the same sort of burns, perhaps even more serious ones. Yet he was a hero—in the minds of his people he was an important person. It did not matter that he was nothing but a glorified servant or hash slinger. His people in Corapeake saw him as a great man who had put his life on the line in the war against Japan. To both black and white citizens, he was coming home as a patriotic American who was fighting to "make the world safe for democracy." Mama Miles had told everybody in town, white and black, that Raymond was coming, so when the Bee pulled into Corapeake on New Year's Eve, it looked as if everybody in Corapeake was there. Even the white editor of the local newspaper was there to get a picture and a story to put on the "colored page" of his paper.

After about an hour of greetings and talking at the train station, Raymond joined some of his friends to walk over to the black side of town for a soda pop and a fish sandwich. Corapeake never changed. Bulldog Johnson was patrolling the streets. The same people were sitting on the benches near the cafe, pool hall, barber shop, hair salon, and grocery store. At the Blueberry Hill juke joint, people still bought bootleg liquor and danced the night away. As Raymond was about to eat his catfish sandwich, he heard the piccolo playing a song which almost took away his appetite. It was the same song he had heard when he was leaving Natchez the last time, called "Natchez Burning" or "The Burning in that Natchez, Mississippi Town," by the Howlin Wolf. The song went like this:

Did you ever hear about the burning,

That happened way down in Natchez, Mississippi town?

Did you ever hear about the burning,

That happened way down in Natchez, Mississippi town

The old building got to burning,

Found my baby laying on the ground.

Charlotte Jones was there.

Luiza was there.

Rosa Mae was there.

Louise was there.

Did you ever hear about the burning,

That happened way down in Natchez, Mississippi town?

I stood back was looking

And the old building done tumbled down.

Mum—mum—mum—mum (Moaning)

This was what Mississippians call the blues, and this whole episode of returning home gave Raymond the blues—the real blues. It has been said more than once that no one can dream up the real blues, nor can you get the blues when you want them. You can only get the blues when personal experiences, both past and present, create a mood or feeling of total involvement—when you are totally lost in situations of life which can only be explained through blues. Whatever the blues were, Raymond knew that he had them.

So Raymond asked a couple of his friends to accompany him to the Blueberry Hill juke joint, and he put a quarter in the piccolo and played the record five times in succession. As the record played, people danced unaware of the meaning of the words of the song. But while "Natchez Burning" was the catalyst which brought on the real blues, Raymond knew that the problem was much larger than the Natchez fire, as devastating as it was. The real blues for black people do not come only from events like the Natchez fire, the lynching of J.C., the evil antics of Bulldog Johnson and the Klan, or the sexual exploitation of Doodle Cates and Sally Mae Cousins. The blues are a constant undercurrent in our society going back to the African slave trade, through slavery, Jim Crow laws, segregation and discrimination, and the creation of a mind-set of acceptance of the white man's injustice by black people. Blacks live daily with the blues—sometimes for so long that they don't even know it anymore. It takes something like "Natchez Burning" to bring feelings to conscious focus.

Raymond now looked at Corapeake and other parts of the world as he knew them through the Navy. He was convinced that Corapeake was not just in Mississippi, but everywhere—from Florida to Maine, from New York to California, from Texas to Hawaii. America never lets black people forget that they are black. So if we must fight in a war, we can't just fight in a white man's war. We must find a way to fight the war at home and create a revolution in the way black people think. Until blacks can attack the systemic causes of the blues, until we can die for the things that make us free, until we are willing to demand freedom for our families and be willing to die for it,

204

there will always be black holocausts—sacrifices of black lives that destroy the black spirit.

As Raymond left the Blueberry to go out to the old home place, he wondered, "How long will Papa's and Mama's God, and mine, continue to let black people go through seemingly unquenchable fires in Mississippi, in Honolulu and fires everywhere, fanned by the cursed winds of racial hate and injustice. How long, O Lord, how long?"